Dark Passages

A Collection of **6** Short Stories
By M.J. PRESTON

Dear Reader,

Thank you for purchasing and reading this small collection of stories. I would like to ask you a favor.

If you enjoy this collection, please leave a review at the place which you purchased it, be it Amazon, Goodreads, Barnes and Noble or even word of mouth. Unlike large publishing houses, independent artists do not have the luxury of an expensive marketing team, so your input is instrumental in keeping independent art alive.

At present independent artists around the world are struggling to bring their art to the public eye. They do not do this simply for monetary gain, but to share with others.

If you like an artist's work, tell others and buy their work so that the artist can continue to create.

Thank you for your support.

M.J. PRESTON

Dedicated
to
Brad Hardy

Long hours, long miles, great conversation.

Authors Note

The stories contained in this book are a work of fiction, any resemblance to persons living or dead is purely coincidental; however, the author has taken the liberty of using historical characters, references and places to enhance the reader experience. Any references to known and convicted criminals, along with political figures have been added to enhance the story and lend realism to the fictional tale contained in this book.

ISBN-13: 978-1523202980
ISBN-10: 152320298X

Stories and Artwork
Copyright © 2016
M.J. PRESTON

Edited by Jake Anfinson

TABLE OF CONTENTS

Introduction

By Jake Anfinson

I met M.J. Preston through WritingForums.com, where I'm a staff member. Being a fan of horror and suspense, I naturally sit up and take notice when I see good reviews about a writer I've never heard of. So when another member posted that The Equinox was a rare gem of excellent characterization (something I'm sure most of you would agree is generally lacking in horror fiction), I headed straight to Amazon to give it a shot.

And I've been pestering him ever since.

Got anything new for me, M.J.?

Come on, crank it out and gimme.

Some of the stories in this collection you may have already read in anthologies. Some may be new to you. I will only suggest that when you do kick back in your comfy chair, or settle in to bed for the night, that you keep a light burning. Have your crucifix at hand, your vials of holy water, a box of silver bullets, and pour salt across your window sills. You can't be too careful. After all, that noise you hear might be something even worse than a skinwalker.

I hope you like these stories as much as I do. Just remember one thing—Preston's muse is a bastard, so be prepared for anything.

Jake Anfinson
01/01/2016

RUN-OFF 31

Run-off 31

Chicago, Illinois
Summer, 2013

The bodies started turning up in late July. Before long, police began to think that this was not the work of one serial killer, but two, possibly even three. The only flaw in this thinking lay in the fact that every victim had been left with an identical incision from solar plexus to belly button. Some of the detectives called them the 'X Killings', because carved into each victim's belly was an 'X' that was not a symbol but the end result of evisceration. The reason they speculated the killings couldn't possibly be committed by one perpetrator the sheer number of victims. To date there were forty-four, and the dead weren't more than a day or two old when they began turning up. Now, into the end of August, meant only one thing: the killer, or killers, were claiming a victim a day on average, with the odd double.

Sean Woodman was not assigned to the case, he wasn't even a cop anymore, but he followed closely through the papers. It reminded him of a case he'd worked back in his days as a Chicago Police Detective. A case that was never closed. He'd been young and cocky back then, but along with his damn-the-torpedoes attitude, he also had a talent for seeing things others missed. And with the exception of that one unsolved case, he'd cleared a lot of murders. Those cleared cases garnished a respect which would eventually pave the way to a door plate which read: Deputy Chief of Police. That was the end of the line for Woodman. He wasn't a cop anymore, just a PR man who practiced politics with the best of them. Truth was, he hated it. He missed the smell of an unsolved case and made it his business to poke his head in on a task force or two to get a whiff of that scent. At first they thought he was some crazy micro-manager from upstairs. But Woodman proved a great help to his fellow officers; and even better, he took zero credit. Word got around, and after a while the task force cops started coming to him for insight.

Chief Jorgenson didn't like it though when Woodman got down in the trenches with the troops. Woodman thought that dislike was born out of resent. Jorgenson had been a career pencil pusher and had no cred with the cops he commanded. Although Jorgenson disapproved, there was no real reason to put a halt to Woodman's actions. Woodman had balanced his position while Deputy Chief with an occasional task force consultation quite well. When a case cleared, the Chief did what any politician would do: He held a press conference, congratulated his officers, and basked unabashedly in their success.

Then the unthinkable happened to Woodman. The unthinkable being, a car accident that resulted in the death of his wife, Jesse. Then there was the trace amount of alcohol in his bloodstream that hardly registered .04 on the breathalyzer. He hadn't blown enough to be charged, he wasn't legally drunk, but Jesse was gone and when word got out, the media hooked onto him like a pariah. They dogged him about the accident, and about how much he'd drank after someone leaked the blood alcohol tests.

His career ended in much the same way Jesse's life had—abrupt and without mercy. He found himself standing before the Mayor and Chief Jorgenson. On either side of them, like book ends, a Public Relations Bitch and the City Lawyer. Set neatly on a table before them, a stack of paper roughly an inch and a half thick.

That's 'The Big Fuck You,' he thought. Somewhere through that he heard the Mayor offering words of regret, and there was even a round of condolence. But it was hollow, the papers on that table spoke more about what was at play than these four assholes put together. In the end he did the only thing he could do. He signed his resignation, took a handsome buyout, and left them to pat each other on the back. That was the end of Sean Woodman's career in the Chicago Police Department. And though he was gone, he never forgot that one big case that got away. The one with the Indian named Blackbird, and the bodies of women they found in the Chicago sewers. They had also been eviscerated, but the bellies of those girls had been torn open. They called the case Little Big Horn, because on the evening of the last murder there had been an exchange of fire which included the use of a cross bow. Considering that Daniel Blackbird had been of Native descent and was the one firing the arrows, the name stuck.

Scott Emmett showed up on Woodman's doorstep with a case file thicker than a city phone book. He liked Emmett, but he was adamant that his days as a cop were over. Emmett was the son-in- law of his partner and best friend, Brad Rosedale. Coincidentally, Rosedale had been a part of that forgotten case as well. Unlike Woodman, Brad moved on. In fact, he moved all the way on down to Tennessee, somewhere between Nashville and Memphis with his third wife.

"I can't do this, Scott. If Jorgenson found out, you were on my doorstep you could find yourself in deep shit. You could lose your job."

"Well, normally I'd say fuck Jorgenson, but to be honest, he sanctioned this visit," Emmett replied.

"Don Jorgenson told you to come see me?"

"Yeah."

Woodman laughed, not because it was funny, but because he couldn't believe the bastard would have the nerve. "Nothing personal, Scott, but you can tell Jorgenson to go fuck himself."

"We need your help, Sean."

"Why should I care? I'm not a cop anymore."

"The last one was a ten-year-old girl."

"Jesus Christ." Woodman sighed and pushed open the screen door. Emmett stepped through the

11

doorway and followed Woodman down the hall of his two room bungalow. "You know that the whole 'last one was a ten-year-old girl' is pretty fucking lame. Little girls get murdered all the time."

"There's something else."

"Yeah, what's that?"

"We have a suspect."

"You've made an arrest? I didn't read anything in the papers."

"No, not exactly, but we...*I* need your help."

"So, you want what? Me to sit down with this guy? Jorgenson can't be agreeing to that. This is all over the papers. I could see the headline— 'High profile case pulls disgraced Deputy Chief out of retirement.' As much as I would love to make that fuck-stick squirm, I still have my daughter to think about."

"How is Stacey?"

"I don't know; she hates my guts. I killed her mother after all."

"There's one other thing, Sean."

"What's that?"

"The suspect says he knows you."

"What? Who is he?"

"He doesn't have a name, but he says he knows you and won't talk to anyone else."

———

They rode in Emmett's car. Woodman leafed through the case file, Emmett briefing him as they rode. "He's approximately forty-years-old, no tattoos and he's huge."

"You mean fat?" Sean was staring at one of the crime scene photos. It was the body of a woman. She was nude, her stomach unzipped.

"No, tall. Stands like seven-foot-three. Scary-looking fucker."

"Where did you pick him up?"

"That's where we're going now."

"How would he know me?"

"I don't know, but we found something."

"What? What did you find?"

Emmett turned toward him, his face serious. "It will be better if you see it. This guy identified you by name. He said you would know him if you met him and he said one other thing." Emmett turned his attention back to the road.

"What?"

"He said, 'I am Number 4.'"

"What? Where? What the fuck? Where the fuck are you taking me?"

"We're going to the run-off." Emmett glanced over then back to the road. "Run-off 31."

Woodman fell silent, but his mind raced. *Run-off 31. Did they? Was it possible? After all these years? Had they*

13

finally caught him. His teeth clenched, turning his cheeks out into hardened contours of meat.

———

Being back down there, plodding through the sewers, sent tremors through Woodman. It wasn't just the claustrophobia, it was the smell, the dripping sounds, and below the pungent order of methane and human waste lay something darker. Woodman thought about the Nazi death camps and the smell associated with them. Real or imagined, those who visited those dark satanic mills associated that smell with death. This place was very much the same and though it had been almost fourteen years, he still recalled the bloated headless corpses in Run-off 31. They got more than they bargained for when they, Chicago PD, went down below. A log jam of bodies, all headless and eviscerated, crammed into that run-off, like...

"Spoils." Rosedale called from the past. "Like a bunch of fucking discarded chicken carcasses."

Up front, Emmett plodded through the sludge, stirring the septic slew with his hip waders, creating a tide of lurching waves that lapped against the scum-coated walls of the underground tunnel. Woodman felt the pressure of the liquid pushing his own waders against his legs. Emmett had come prepared.

"You boys are going to bring the suspect through this shit, seriously?"

Emmett stopped, swung about, the beam of his flashlight gliding across the glistening walls. Facing

Woodman, he said. "He's already there."

"I thought you said that you guys had him in custody."

"Not exactly. He's contained."

"What the fuck is up here, Emmett?"

Emmett chewed his lower lip, eyes losing focus momentarily. Then his gaze hardened and he turned to continue on. "It will be better if I show you." Woodman considered protesting, but his curiosity had the better of him and at this point complaining would accomplish little, if anything. So, he did the only thing he could do; he followed the young officer and they continued on toward the run-off.

They reached the mouth ten minutes later. The arch of concrete was a little over eight feet high. This section of the sewer was as old as the city itself, the walls pitted and worn, falling victim to the elements and toxicity of gas vapors. Emmett halted, tracing the beam of light up the wall until it fell upon a rectangular plate stamped out of brass that had long since faded and turned green.

It read: RUN-OFF 31.

Woodman didn't need the sign. This place was etched into his memory. Through that archway, thirty feet ahead bobbed the horrific memory of his cold case.

"Are you ready?" Emmett's gaze was neutral, even distant.

"Yeah, let's do this."

They waded forward; sloshing liquid bounced off the conduit walls, announcing their presence to the subterranean wildlife. A rat scurried along the edge and dove into the slew, dog-paddling away from them. Thirty feet in Woodman stopped, listening for the ghosts of his past, wondering if they were watching him now. Emmett said nothing, waiting patiently for the moment of silence to pass. It did and Woodman whispered, "Let's go."

Sixty feet in, they came to a Y-Junction. To the left, the run-off continued its course to wherever it was the water flowed. To the right, the path began to climb out of the murky liquid. At its base slimy cobble awaited, but farther up it looked dry. The archway was still high enough to walk upright and for this Woodman was thankful. His back was thankful as well.

"What do you make of this?"

Scrawled into the cobble by their feet was a single word: CHARON. The inscription was not old, weeks, perhaps as long as a month, and it was done free-hand, chiseled into the cobblestone and blotted with what looked to be blood.

Woodman studied it, something in that name struck a chord, but he couldn't put his finger on it. "I don't know. Could it be the name of your Perp?"

"No, I don't think so."

"Okay, that's it! What in the name of fuck is going

on here? First you tell me you want me to speak to a suspect, then you drag me down into the sewers. Now I'm taken back to the scene of an old case and you've been...well, *cryptic* seems to be the operative word."

Emmett's gaze was trained upon him, but he said nothing.

"Okay that's it!" Woodman swung around, ready to wade back into the septic stream.

"Wait."

He stopped.

"Almost everything I told you is true, Sean. We need your help."

His back still turned, Woodman responded. "You want my help. Start talking."

"Okay."

He pivoted back around to face Emmett. "I'm waiting."

Emmett took a long, deliberate breath then exhaled. "We tracked our suspect here this afternoon after the body of a ten-year-old girl turned up in St. Paul Woods. This was a fresh kill—crime scene puts it down to hours. The mother wasn't even aware yet that the daughter was missing, let alone dead. She's a latchkey kid, with a single mom working two jobs. Some old homeless guy picking bottles and cans came across her, and he saw the murder."

"He didn't intervene?"

"As I said before, the Perp is huge, I don't think our witness could have done much."

"Never mind, carry on."

"The old man, he's a mess. He said that the girl was screaming when the ghoul cut her open. Screaming and begging for her life." Emmett stopped, took another deep breath and then continued. "So, when it's over, the old guy says the Perp removed her organs and put them into some kind of carry bag then starts out across the park. The homeless guy decides to follow, albeit at a fair distance, but God love him for showing some balls. He follows the Perp out of St. Paul over to Oakton Street all the way into Skokie. Two fucking miles, Sean. Guess where it leads him?"

Woodman said, "Little Big Horn."

"You got it. Same place your guy was dumping bodies down the sewer. Same alley. Same fucking manhole. Except this guy pulls back the manhole cover and goes down the hole like a fucking...what did they call those underground moles in H.G. Wells' *The Time Machine*?"

"Morlocks?"

"Yeah like a fucking Morlock. Not far from there, there's a community Precinct. After the Perp goes down the hole, the old guy makes for the Precinct. Takes him about twenty minutes to convince the community cop he's not a loon, twenty more to locate the body, and another ten to call us. We were mobile within an hour and a half. I figured he was long gone.

Then, on a hunch I decided to check the Run-off. That's where we found him. Where he is now."

"Why isn't he in the tombs under lock and key?"

"Because we don't have him in custody. We just have him cornered."

Anger bubbled up. "Cornered! You brought me to an apprehension? I don't even have a gun! What the fuck is the matter with you!"

Emmett reached into his jacket and produced a Desert Eagle 9 mm. "You can have this if it makes you feel better, but you won't need it. He's behind some kind of plexus-glass barrier."

"Barrier?"

"Sean, please. Come with me, it's only another sixty yards. He says he knows you. Says that he is Number 4, he won't talk to anyone but you. The others are waiting. We've got 10 armed cops down there, and you have my spare gun. I need you to talk to this guy, he's up to something, but I'm not sure what. I can stand here and debrief you for another hour, but it will be easier if you just follow me the rest of the way."

"Is it the man from Little Big Horn? Do you think this is my guy?"

"I really don't know. That's for you to decide."

Both men carried on into the darkness.

———

"This is Detective Emmett! I am entering the scene with former Deputy Chief Sean Woodman!" Emmett shifted impatiently from one foot to the other. "Answer, God damn it!"

"Okay Detective, it's clear for you to enter."

The light at the end opened up into a pumping station that had been cut in half by a barrier that indeed looked like plexus-glass. On one side, strategically positioned, police officers stood, weapons drawn and at the ready. On the other, a lone silhouette sat staring out at his captors over a sea of clay pottery. The lighting was dim, but Woodman caught the grin that suddenly formed on the stranger's face and knew that this sudden show of pleasure was due mostly to his arrival.

"What the fuck is he doing here," Woodman cussed when he saw Jorgenson walking toward him.

"I'm sorry, Sean, I didn't think you'd come if I told you."

"You're right, I wouldn't have."

"Thank you for coming, Sean," Chief Jorgenson stuck out his hand.

Woodman turned his attention from Emmett to Jorgenson. "Put it away, Jorg, I'm not shaking your fucking hand," he said then, raising his voice just slightly, added, "Would I be correct to assume that that pottery contains what was taken from the victims?"

"Yeah, that would be correct." Jorgenson lowered his hand and placed it into his pocket. He took a cursory glance around to see if his subordinates had noticed; they had.

"How did he get in there?"

"We don't know."

Then from behind. "Wood Man."

Startled, Woodman pivoted to face the Perp.

He rose, strode forward, coming into the light. He was a giant of a man. His hands hung like machinery at his sides. His clothes, still stained with copper, gave testament to the last killing. His face was hard and angular, bone and muscle pulled his skin back making him look gaunt.

"I have been waiting for you?"

"You have? Why?"

"Because you have seen him."

"Who?"

"Keh Run, of course."

"I don't know any Keh Run. Who are you?"

"I am Number 4."

"How did you get in there? Who is Keh Run?"

The stranger frowned. "I do not like games, Wood Man."

Woodman thought back to the inscription in the cobblestone. Charon. "Was that his name at the base of the tunnel? I thought it was pronounced Charon, not Keh Run."

"Yes, Charon." He smiled again, revealing uniform planks of yellow teeth, looking more like old fence boards stacked on top of each other. He folded his hands neatly in front him, tilting his head downward.

"You said you knew me." Woodman decided to ask the question that was eating him alive. "Have you done this before? Back in 2001? Was that you?" He brought his eyes up to meet the stranger, steeling his expression and waiting.

The stranger's smile melted back into his milky complexion. He turned and moved back between the pots, settling down on his pedestal; arms crossed. From there, shadows fell upon his face, making it look skull-like.

"What now?" Emmett whispered.

Woodman cocked his head right, catching Jorgenson and Emmett's attention and glanced toward the opening of the pump room. They took the hint and followed. Once out of earshot, he began talking. "This isn't my guy."

"How can you be sure?"

"The girls back in 2001 were torn open, their heads literally twisted off. This wacko is emulating that, but he wouldn't know the state the victims were in. Does anyone have a cell phone that works down here?"

Emmett pulled out his iPhone. "Yeah, I have a

signal."

"Okay, google Charon."

From above, a muddy drop of water fell downward and splashed across the screen.

"Fuck." He wiped it with his sleeve or he tried to then stopped. "It's going to take a second, the touch screen doesn't react well to liquid poo."

Woodman and Jorgenson both laughed, but stifled their amusement when they saw the other sharing in the joke. "So what's your contingency plan?" Woodman asked.

"I've got a SWAT team coming down with a fixed charge. If you can't talk him out, we'll go tactical and take the fucker out." Jorgenson nudged Emmett. "How are you making out?"

"Give me a second, the signal is pretty weak."

"There has to be another way in. Are you looking at that?"

"I've got a city works guy coming with blue prints, but these are some old fucking tunnels. When I called over the Chief of Operations he asked me if I was kidding. Said that finding a blue-print of this section might take a lot of hours."

"But he found them?"

"Yeah, he's conferring with the SWAT Lieutenant."

"Got it! Holy shit, if this is right, this dude has

some serious expectations of you, Sean."

Woodman reached over, took the phone and began to read. He didn't have his glasses, but the font was large enough that he didn't struggle too much. After he finished, he passed the phone over to Jorgenson and said, "Well, at least we know who Charon is."

"He's certifiable," Jorgenson said.

"Really? You needed Google to figure that out, eh, Jorg? The whole evisceration thing didn't tip you off?" Woodman regretted letting that out only a second after it spilled from his mouth. Bitterness would accomplish nothing here.

Jorgenson glanced up, his face red and angry. "You don't want to be here. I'll have an officer escort you out. I didn't end your career, you did."

"Could we save this for another time?" Emmett interrupted.

Woodman didn't give Jorgenson a chance to respond. He walked out of the pump room back to the plexus. "The boatman. You're waiting for the boatman to arrive?"

The stranger rose. "Charon, yes. I have a tidy sum to give him."

"Who are you?"

"I told you, I am Number 4." He reached down and lifted the lid from one of the pots. "One left to fill then Charon will come for me."

"What is this? Why did you ask for me?"

The stranger smiled. "You will see."

From behind, Jorgenson whispered, "I just got word, they found another tunnel that'll lead them in. Tactical will be here in five, keep him talking."

"Why do you call yourself Number 4?"

"Because I am not the first." He stood, walked to the back of the enclosure. "I am the fourth servant, cast down to earth. But to find my way back to the Master, I must first do his bidding and payment must be made."

"Payment to Charon?"

From behind, Jorgenson again. "Four minutes."

"Yes, but he is also a servant. He will take my payment, but the cargo will not be his to keep." The stranger reached up onto the wall and flicked a switch. The room lit up, shadows retreating into the walls and in their absence Woodman saw it all.

There behind him, amongst the many clay pots smeared with copper that could only be coagulant, formed a new source of concern. Was it? Beneath a tarpaulin standing upright was a figure that could only be...

"Behold, Wood Man!" The stranger said and pulled away the tarp.

Horror cut through him like rusty barb wire. Woodman's eyes widened, his thoughts spinning and as shock melted over him he could hear himself screaming. "No! No! No! No!"

From behind, Jorgenson again. Panicked. "Keep him talking. Tactical is close."

"Stacey!"

She was barely conscious, not a strip of clothing on her body, her arms tied behind her back, her belly exposed. Like a witch on a stake.

"Jesus Christ, no! Let her go, please."

"Forty-five is the number, Wood Man."

There below her, a pot was waiting, its lid removed.

The officers at the scene raised their weapons. Safeties clicked off.

The stranger reached down and produced a knife, its blade long and curving into a hook. He stepped forward and blew into her face. "Wake, child."

"You fucking psycho, let her go!" Woodman was blubbering. "Please, take me instead!"

Suddenly conscious, Stacey whimpered, "Daddy?"

"It's time, Wood Man." He grinned and raised the blade.

"Shoot! Shoot the fucker!" Jorgenson ordered.

The underground room exploded in a barrage of gunfire. Bullets ricocheted off the plexus, one zipping past Woodman's head. Another struck Jorgenson in the throat opening his jugular. Blood spurted out of the wound, splashing upward against the plexus; first defying gravity then it began to flow downward. Another officer was struck in the ankle, bone fragments splintered from skin in porcupine fashion.

The stranger seemed not to notice.

Woodman begged—pleaded—cried and then fell to his knees when the knife cut up into her belly on its first diagonal pass. Stacey stiffened, her eyes locking with her father's. Then, after the second cut, she screamed, but only for a second; the peal drowned out by her father's howls of anguish.

Emmett ordered, "Hold your fire! Hold your fire!" Then a bullet cut into his guts, turning his knees to rubber. As if in prayer, he dropped and let loose a groan that exemplified agony.

Woodman could only hope a stray bullet would take him, but the barrage fell silent, replaced by ringing disbelief. Stacey's chin rested against her chest, her mouth opening and closing, her pupils dilating.

Take her, please take her now, Woodman prayed.

Then, with one hooked hand, the stranger who called himself Number 4 reached inside to eviscerate her. She was gone before the audible plop, her insides warming the cool clay jar.

The stranger came to the glass, and with one bloodied finger wrote the word: Charon.

"Your soul for hers," he invited.

"You bastard, you fucking psycho piece of shit!"

From the headset that now lay beside a dead Jorgenson, he heard, "One minute to breach!"

27

The stranger returned to the center of the pots and stood on his pedestal. Then he began to pray aloud in some foreign tongue. It was rhythmic, rising and falling. Woodman had never heard the language, but it was indeed a language.

"You're going to get the needle for this, you sick fuck!"

"*Shay-gra-che-Keh-Run-la-a-Jee*," he prayed, a chant of psychobabble. "*Keh Run-la-a-Jee! Charon! La-a-jee! Charon! La-a-jee!*"

Something began to happen.

From each pot a light began to bloom, first growing then pulsing like a heartbeat. All of them, all forty-five glowed in a myriad of color. The temperature plummeted, frost forming on the walls, turning breath into vapor.

"What's happening?" someone asked.

The stranger began to change as well. His face hardening, the milky skin turning first to serape and then ashen. The radiance from the pots increased, the stranger raised a hand, his skin crumbling away like cigarette ash leaving only an accusing boney talon. "Behold," he said.

Behind him, the wall began to ripple and then fade. Light dissolved the matrix of reality and the wall was no more. Reality buckled and came apart. A corridor materialized; a long wide passageway set in stone bookmarking each side, halfway filled with water. Down that passage was a place that those who feared for their eternal soul would not dare look.

Woodman, mouth agape, remembered what he'd read: *Dark and dismal, the River of Acheson and across the Styx cometh the boatman: Charon to collect the payment for safe passage to Hades.*

The light inside each of the pots rose and materialized corporeally.

First he saw a man, then woman, then a child, and then Stacey. Behind them, the stranger continued to decompose, muscle degenerating, skin tightening, until only mummified bone remained.

"Oh my God," the officer whose ankle had been shot called out.

Down the corridor, pushing against the current, the boatman was coming.

The ghostly forms gathered about the one who called himself Number 4 and followed him to the shoreline as the boatman approached.

"Hades," Woodman mumbled.

"What?" Emmett grunted.

"Your soul for hers," he had offered.

There's still time. I can save her. I can stop him from taking her!

Woodman reached into his jacket pocket, felt the gun, wrapped his fingers around the pistol grip. "I can't let this happen! I can't let him take her!"

Almost at the shore now, soon the boatman would

be ready to take them aboard.

"Sean! What are you doing?" Emmett cried.

Sean Woodman placed the gun barrel under his chin, closed his eyes and squeezed.

———

Revelation Lamb

He tapped on the passenger window and the driver lowered it. "Yeah?"

"Special Agent Webster." He flipped open his identification. "Dunleavy sent me. You Perron?"

The man inside the car nodded. "Yeah." He hit the lock release. "Get in." As he climbed in Perron remarked, "Didn't take long for someone to get here."

"I was just down the road, in Weedsport, visiting my sister when the Albany office called. Dunleavy said you called; needed a backup."

"Did they tell you anything else?"

"They were pretty vague other than to say: 'Homegrown Terrorist' —and that it was high priority. They needed someone here pronto." He shrugged. "I guess I was the closest."

"Sorry to interrupt your dinner."

"No sweat. We were finished when I got the call."

"Where's your wheels, Webster?"

I parked around back. I didn't want to compromise you."

"I appreciate that, but you're early. He hasn't arrived yet."

"Good, then you can bring me up to speed."

Perron exhaled, reached into the back seat and grabbed a file folder. He opened it and tapped his index finger on a black and white surveillance photo clipped to the first page of the report. "John Lamb. He was recruited into the Revelation Church about two years ago. He's single, unemployed, possibly a bit on the schizophrenic side, so very easily influenced."

Webster took it from him. The name at the top of the report caught his eye before he even looked at the picture. It read: Horseman. "I've heard about this, they've been talking about this. He's your Unsub?" Unsub was short for Unknown Subject. Not only had Webster heard about this unidentified suspect, he'd also heard of the Horseman, but only second hand in the Albany Bureau and it had been strained through a filter before reaching his ears. The Horseman file was far above his security clearance. He was suddenly excited; this could be a career changing take-down. Then he examined the picture. In it, an average-looking man, mid-30's, with a horseshoe of dark hair that encircled the crown of his bald head. He was dressed in blue jeans and a t-shirt and it looked as though he was standing outside a government building. "He's the Horseman?"

"Yeah," Perron lit a cigarette and offered one to Webster.

"No thanks, gave them up a few years back." He turned his attention back to the photo. "John Lamb."

"Fitting name for a man intent on bringing about the Armageddon."

Webster glanced up from the file "Listen, I'm on a bit of an information curve here. Can you fill me in?"

"Sure, I'll give you the Readers Digest version, but if he rolls in you'll have to wait for the rest."

"Fair enough." Webster could feel his pulse, along with his mind, racing. *Bio-terrorism! This was unbelievable.*

"About eight months ago a lab in Ypsilanti Michigan was broken into and approximately 500 ml of a germ agent labeled T740YA was stolen. 'YA' for short. The official story is that this stuff was intercepted by the Israeli's during the run-up to the second Gulf War. A group of Jihadists were transporting this bio-agent across the border from Syria when a Kidon Force neutralized the entire show."

"Kidon?"

"Yeah, they're supposed to be an elite Israeli assassination force. Their version of black ops, but according to the Israeli's, Kidon doesn't exist. Anyhow, a group sanctioned by the Syrians were shipping this stuff in to use on our troops when the Jews cut the operation off below the waist."

Webster shook his head. "Okay, but how did we end up with this stuff in our backyard?"

Perron ignored the question, lowered the driver window and tossed his smoke out. "Up until a week ago this must have been super top secret, because the Lab in Ypsilanti was being fronted by another company called: Hydro-Cast Structural. According to their profile, Hydro-Cast was in the business of making pre-fab foundations. But that was just a front because in the basement of that place was a fully operational government grade bio-lab. It appeared that Hydro-Cast Structural had another mandate. Bio-weapons defense."

Webster shook his head and laughed. "Defense, yeah sure."

"Who knows? Defense or not, a rather moot point at this stage, because the germ that was stolen— 'YA'—very nasty stuff. Worse than anything you can imagine. It makes Ebola plague look like the common cold. It immediately incubates on touch. Which is to say, that if you get even a drop of it on your skin it absorbs and turns you into a walking talking petre dish in less than an hour?"

"Shit," Webster said.

"Shit isn't the half of it. Once this stuff incubates it mutates into an airborne virus in less than a day of finding a host. So every breath becomes highly infectious. The host doesn't have to cough or spit on another person, they just have to breathe in close proximity. That's all it takes. Become infected and go into a subway station and you pass it to the people sitting close. In an hour they are also infected, and within a day they are passing it along in the exact same way."

"Is there an antidote?"

"None that I'm aware, but like you I'm just a foot soldier. So the stock answer is: I don't know."

"This stinks, Perron. What is a Laboratory in Ypsilanti Michigan doing with an extremely volatile bio-weapon that has the ability to wipe out an entire population in such a short time?"

"You already said that. That's the official story, but I'm guessing that folks well above our pay grade know where this shit really came from. My main concern isn't whether the spooks are massaging us with bullshit. My primary concern is Mr. Lamb, who, according to my source, is on his way here to plant the first seed."

"So what's the plan?"

"Initially clearance was given to neutralize on sight with extreme prejudice, but there's been a new development. My source says there are four Horsemen."

"Three more guys like this?"

"Yeah."

"Why didn't Dunleavy say something to me?"

"This didn't come from the Bureau, it came from a C.I. that I have working in the field. I've been tracking this guy for the better part of six months. My source on the inside told me that Lamb was getting second thoughts, maybe even getting ready to flip. If that is the case, I need to take him alive because we have three other threats out there and I don't have to tell you, Agent Webster, that it is very likely that they are working in unison to carry out a coordinated four-prong strike."

"So what's the plan then?"

———

John Lamb squeezed the steering wheel as he rolled eastbound on the New York Thruway. *This is wrong,* he thought, but didn't dare say it aloud. *How did I get myself into this?* He was sweating profusely, he felt nauseous, and just ahead, driving it all home, a sign read: **NY THRUWAY SERVICE AREA 2 MILES AHEAD** *Take a Safety Break!*

He eased off on the accelerator. How he'd allowed them take complete control and worst of all, how he was going to get out of this. *There is no getting out of it. Jasper's eyes are everywhere. He sees everything. He will know.* But would he? John wasn't so sure now, his head had begun to clear and the words that the Reverend Jasper Sherman had crafted and delivered so graciously now seemed venomous and ugly.

———

The car pulled into the lot. Perron eased up in his seat, focusing on the sedan, trying to decide. Once he was sure he said, "That's him."

Webster wasn't aware that he was holding his breath, he could feel his chest tightening, sudden waves of apprehension washing over him. *This guy is here to seed it. Oh my god! Oh my god!*

"You're sure it's him?"

"Positive." Perron pulled out his service pistol, attached a silencer and cocked it. "I'm going to try and take him alive, but if I get any indication that he won't come cooperatively, I'm going to neutralize him on the spot."

Lamb parked the car and shut the lights off. He was directly across from them, taillights to the rear. Webster pulled out his own weapon. He didn't have a silencer, but then he'd never been sent to neutralize anyone. Lamb was getting out of his car now, moving toward the trunk.

"Oh fuck, he's going for it," Webster gasped.

Perron reached over and unlocked the door. Then the unthinkable happened. A mini-van pulled in right beside Lamb's car. On the back, an annoying stick figure family of five. A Mom, a Dad and three little ones. "Damn it. Not now, not fucking now!"

Webster let out an exasperated sigh. "He's opening the trunk."

"I can see that."

"We got to take him out, Perron."

Perron turned to Webster. "Not yet."

The lights on the min-van shut off and the passenger door opened first. Out stepped who they presumed was the mother, then the driver door, and Mom opened the sliding door on the side. They began unloading their kids; all three of them.

Lamb was standing with his back to them, opening the trunk. The family was rallying between the vehicles only a few feet away from him, oblivious to the danger. Lamb was reaching into the trunk now and Webster seemed ready to pounce. He reached for the door handle and Perron caught his arm before he could pull it open.

"Agent Webster, what do you think you're doing?"

"We gotta take him down."

"Not yet, we go in guns blazing and I don't think I have to tell you what the outcome will be."

Webster was aghast. "If he seeds that fucking virus, one family won't matter!" He was tugging at his arm, trying to pull away. For the first time in a long time, Webster was afraid. "Let me go."

"Get a grip on yourself," Perron snapped. "I'm not stupid, I know the consequences, but there are three more out there. If I plug him without at least trying to get those names it will all be for nothing."

Webster pulled his arm free then shook his head angrily. "Well then, what's the fucking plan?"

Perron looked out the windshield. Lamb had a carry bag in his hand now, he was looking around suspiciously. The family was getting ready to go inside. "Too risky to take him down in the parking lot. Too many people around."

"He's on the move! Whatever you're thinking spit it out or I'm going after him alone!"

Perron watched Lamb, he was following closely behind the family as they ambled across the parking lot. He was looking around again, using them for cover. "Okay, I'll shadow him in. If I can get him alone, I'll try and take him alive. If not, I'll shoot him where he stands."

"What do you want me to do?"

"You stay here. If he comes out, it means I failed. Take him down and call in the cavalry."

"You want me to call the Bureau in Albany? I thought the cavalry was already coming?"

Perron reached into his jacket and pulled out a cell phone. "I don't have a lot of time, so I'm going to be blunt. This here isn't a regular cell phone, it's a transmitter. You press the asterisk three times and then get the hell out of here."

"What? Why?"

"There's a drone circling overhead right now." Perron was talking rapidly, never taking his eyes from Lamb.

"A drone?" Webster's hand was shaking. "You're fucking kidding me right."

"It's will carry out a strike on the facility if I fail to stop him from seeding the virus. It's carrying incendiary explosive, enough to vaporize any infection. You see Lamb leave that building without me and you press * * *—then you've got maybe 15 seconds to get clear." Perron opened the door.

Webster felt like he was going to throw up. "Since when is the Bureau using drones?"

"I never said I work for the Bureau," Perron said. "I'm CIA."

Perron climbed from the vehicle and looked back before closing the door. "Watch that door Agent Webster. I'm counting on you."

———

He jogged across the parking lot, tucking the M9 he was carrying into the waistband of his pants. When he reached the glass door of the service center he spotted Lamb walking into the washroom.

That must be where he intends to set the seed. That's where I'd do it, he mused. *He sure isn't wasting any time.*

When Lamb entered the washroom he was met by a man and his teenage son. They were standing side by side at the urinals. After finishing up they went to the sinks to wash and shared a joke about something. The teenager laughed at what his father was saying. Lamb had no idea what the exchange was about, they could have been shouting directly into his ear and he wouldn't have heard. He was too wrapped up in what he was about to do.

Lord God. Please give me a sign!

The father touched his index finger to the hand dryer and its motor came alive filling the hollow room with mechanical white noise. His son went over to the other dryer and it fired into action doubling the chorus. Now they raised their voices above the dueling hand dryers, while the seemingly invisible Lamb stepped into one of the toilet stalls.

———

He met the father and son exiting the bathroom and looked around to see if anyone else was coming toward the room. To his left there was a yellow folding plastic sign. It read: [CLOSED FOR CLEANING] Poking his head around the corner he checked if anyone else was in there. *No one, just Lamb. Good.* He grabbed the folding sign, set in front of the entrance and stepped inside.

———

Seated on a toilet, Lamb unzipped the carry bag and removed the bottle inside. It was small, not much bigger than a salt shaker with an aerosol pump on top. "One spray will do the trick, don't waste it." Jasper had instructed.

He was having second thoughts. If he did this what would be the consequence? Not just here on earth, but the eternal. He carefully examined the pump bottle and pondered how a god of love could be vengeful and angry enough to destroy all that he had created. That was when he realized he was no longer alone.

Beyond the stall door he heard a zipper being turned down. A second later, the unmistakable sound that could only be a stream of urine beating against the porcelain wall. The drain in the urinal came to life gurgling. This went on for about 20 seconds, slowing to a gradual trickle. Lamb replaced the pump bottle back into the carry-on-bag and slowly zipped it up.

He wouldn't do this. Couldn't. He'd turn himself into the police, suffer the full wrath of the law, but he would not kill. *I would rather be damned,* he thought.

He waited for the man to finish.

The man at the urinal zipped. His shoes squeaked on the tile floor as he made his way to the sink. The automatic taps clicked on, and the sound of flowing water seemed to go on forever. He clutched the bag in his lap, suddenly feeling claustrophobic.

Hurry up, damn you!

The tap shut off and instead of walking to the air dryer he heard the footsteps approach the stall. In the crack at the base of the stall, two slightly worn running shoes settled side by side in front of the door.

"John Lamb," ordered the man on the other side of the door.

Who is he? Police? Government agents?

"I wasn't going to do it. I changed my mind," he whimpered.

"That's good. I have a gun trained on you right now. I will not hesitate to shoot and even through this door it is likely I will hit you. Place the bag on the floor and slide it toward me, then unlatch the door."

Lamb lifted the bag from his lap and set it down on the floor in front of the toilet.

"Okay, now using your foot, push the bag out."

He gave it a push and the man on the other side pulled it under.

"Good, now unlatch the door."

His hand shaking, he reached up and slid the bolt over. The man on the other side pushed the door open and there they were facing each other.

Perron did not look like an agent at all. He wore blue jeans, a Utica College pullover, with a mustard stain just to the left of the U for authenticity. His face, slightly pudgy, was full of summer freckles. His hair, dark with natural curls, was neatly cut. In his hand, an M9 pointed toward the floor. On the muzzle, a silencer.

"God gives us free will, I couldn't do it." Lamb smiled.

Perron raised the gun and opened fire. The reports were low, without drama. **Ponk—Ponk—Ponk.** Those three pops were followed by the spray of blood and brain matter painting the cubicle wall. John Lamb snapped back and then lurched to the left, his right cheek pressing against the cubicle wall, the smile permanently etched into his face.

Replacing the gun in his waistband, Perron reached into his pocket and produced a small tube of super glue. He squeezed a few drops into the jamb. Pulling the stall door closed, he held it until he was sure it had bonded.

He picked up the bag and walked over to the sinks, setting it up onto the counter. Putting on a surgical mask and gloves he sprayed the start buttons on both hand dryers. Finished that, he removed the gloves and mask, placed them into the bag and zipped it. Standing before the mirror he checked himself for anything that might be incriminating. There was nothing.

He grinned. *Good.*

But there was still business.

He'd have to kill Webster when he got back to the car. He reminded himself to make sure he got the cell phone back first. This made him snicker. That had been a sweet piece of improvisation. A drone flying overhead waiting to take out an entire service center. After killing Webster he'd have to put his body in the trunk with the real Perron. He wondered if Bureau vehicles had GPS tracking and decided they probably did. Maybe he'd give the two agents a spray before taking off. He removed his other cell phone and hit the speed dial.

"It's done. I'm going to need a ride."

He exited the washroom. Stopped and moved the [Closed for Cleaning] sign away from the door. There, waiting at the door, were two young boys. Definitely brothers—the oldest eleven—the younger maybe nine. They looked anxious, the youngest shifting from foot to foot. The kid had to pee.

He smiled at them.

"Don't forget to wash your hands."

————

PASSION

Passion

Ypres, France
24 April, 1915

He stumbled through the poisonous fog, face burning, and blind in one eye. The inside of his head was hammering after the exposure to the chlorine gas. The field was littered with bodies, the earth septic with blood and decay. His weapon, which he'd used only moments before to kill advancing enemy, now hung from his sling and dug into his shoulder.

"Momma," Came the deathly cry of a young soldier.

How far off, he wondered.

And again. "Momma?"

That way.

He trudged—as cross-winds dispersed the gas—pushing toward the voice of the wounded soldier. As he walked he thought of his brothers, Frances and Jean Paul, and wondered where they were in the scheme of the battle. Probably dead. He almost cried, but even a single convulsive hiccup set about grating tiny shards of glass in his throat. Then his attention was diverted.

"Mum." The voice was weaker now, the soldier dying or losing strength. There was an air of hopelessness in that cry.

He glanced around, taking in the carnage with his good eye. The field was littered with bodies. Both friend and foe, left in various states of mutilated revulsion. There really was nobody left alive, just himself and that calling voice out here in the purgatory of no man's land.

The blasts of artillery were mere echoes in his mind now. Regimental Fire Missions and their continual barrages upon the enemy machine guns, in an attempt to suppress them. When the howitzers fell silent the canisters began to pop one by one, spewing forth gray green smoke, rolling through the trenches and it only took moments before the men began to climb out and run. Many asphyxiated right there in the trenches and fell dead. Thinking quickly, he abandoned his hole and ran headlong into no man's land, away from the strangling vapor. Around him, they fell, cries of desperation. An officer, in obvious agony, removed his sidearm and shot himself in the temple.

"Piss in a rag," someone yelled. "Cover your mouths."

His eyes were burning and his face and nostrils felt like they'd been immersed in bleach, but he had gotten clear of the worst. As the winds dispersed the gas, he removed a field dressing from his pack and urinated onto the rag. It barely had enough in his bladder to fill a tea cup, but it would have to do. Then he brought it to his face and that gave some relief. The smell of urea, although unpleasant, was better than the burning chlorine. He knelt that way, breathing in, tasting the salt and ammonia, and realizing he had been the one to call out the warning about pissing in a rag.

He got up on his feet and began walking, his bearings askew. As far as he knew, he could be marching straight into the barbed wire and machine guns of the Hun, but then the voice had called out and he began in that direction.

"Mummmmm." The voice, now much closer, called again now very close.

He continued in that direction, using his good eye to scan the scorched landscape. With the gas almost gone, he spotted the silhouette lurching over about twenty feet away and moved to it.

The soldier was badly blistered, his eyes watered from the gas. Beside him his mask sat useless. "Momma."

"Soldier," he said kneeling down beside him. "Can you hear me?"

The soldier looked through him, lifting one bloodied hand to wave at that which he could not see while using the other to prop himself up. "Who's there? It hurts, I want to go home."

"I know it hurts. I was burned by the gas too. What is your name?" He set down his rifle, unbuttoned his scabbard, then kneeled in front of the wounded soldier. "Where are you from?"

"Stephane." Answering a question put the wounded man at ease. "I am from the south shore of Longueuil, Montreal. Who are you?" His eyes were a patchwork of red blotches, his uniform covered in bits of dried mud that stank of cordite. Still, through all of this he managed a smile for his new-found friend.

"Hello Stephane, I am also from Montreal, I grew up in Verdun. I have two brothers out here somewhere, probably among the dead now."

"I'm sorry to hear that. So many have died out here, it all seems so senseless."

"I got lost in the attack. Do you know which way it is back to the friendly lines?"

Stephane lifted a shaking hand and pointed. "That way, the Hun's lines are behind me."

The soldier looked in the direction Stephane was pointed. If he had stayed the course he would have definitely marched right into the German lines. "What were you doing up here?"

"FOO. I was calling in the artillery."

The soldier removed his bayonet and asked, "What did you do before you joined the infantry?"

"I... I was a carpenter. Cabinet maker," he said trying to get up. "I think I can walk. Can you take me to an aid station?"

"Not yet. I, we, my brothers and I worked below the city in the sewers, but that wasn't our passion. Was cabinetry your passion Stephane?"

"I... I suppose, but I don't think it will be now."

"No, no it won't," he chuckled to himself not sharing the joke. "Every man must have a passion. For some it is art, and others like yourself, it is carpentry. For my brothers and I, it was the hunt."

Stephane let out a weak laugh, and said, "What could you possibly hunt in Montreal?"

He joined him in his laughter. "We hunted people, Stephane. Bakers, plumbers, bums, whoever was available. It was our passion."

"You're making a joke at my expense."

"Oh no, no joke."

"I did not get your name."

The soldier continued, ignoring the question. "We signed up for the war and we've been killing every day now. We thought it would be easy to kill in a place where death is so widespread, but it isn't as simple as one might think. We've killed at least fourteen men since coming to France and that doesn't include the Hun." He positioned the bayonet.

"Who are you? What is your name?" Stephane's voice began to rise and fill with fear. "Please..."

"I am death," he said and then plunged the bayonet into Stephane's heart. There was no struggle, nor fanfare, just a burping gasp as the last bit of life expelled from his body.

The soldier withdrew the sacrificial blade, wiped it clean and then sheathed it into the scabbard. He took in his kill, Stephane, the cabinet maker from the south shore. A drop of blood seeped out of his nose, falling into the poisoned mud. He was alone now. Perhaps he would join his brothers in Hades, but for now he would go back and try and find his unit.

He marched toward the friendly trenches...

———

The Children

of

Romani Phoneutria

The Children of Roma Phoneutria

Tuesday

"Goddamn, what the fuck does this woman not understand?" Dan was standing at the apartment door, his face screwed into a knot of frustration. Below his wife, Heather, was at the foot of the concrete stairwell, a clipboard dangling from her right hand. As he continued she tapped the clipboard against her thigh. "I said four o'clock, what the fuck is so hard about that?"

"Maybe she forgot," Heather said, but she really didn't believe it. She continued tapping the clipboard against her thigh, trying to smile, trying to cool Dan's jets. They were done for the day and if he went home in a shit mood the whole night would be a write-off. They'd been doing annual inspections, all fifty-two units, and they were done; except this one. The tenant had been dodging them for weeks. Either feigning sickness or saying she had other commitments; like work. Both Heather and Dan figured the place must be a dump and she was avoiding the inevitable.

"That's it! I'm calling her tonight and if she doesn't comply I'm going in with the master key!" He marched down the short stairwell and pushed passed his wife. "Come on, let's go."

Heather followed, feeling a sting of anger as she tried to catch up. He could be so insensitive, leaving her to trail behind; embroiled in his private tantrum. Dan just couldn't get it through his head—he wasn't in the army anymore—people didn't just come to the chow when you snapped your fingers. When she got up by his side she had to stretch out her legs to keep pace. She wondered if he was doing this on purpose.

"What," he said, reading the anger in her face.

"Nothing, but you can't just barge in. You'll have to check with Murray and I don't think he'll want you entering the unit unaccompanied. Not after that last complaint."

"Fuck, Heather, you going to bring that up again? I didn't take anything!"

"I never said you did, anyway it doesn't matter what I think. That last complaint is on record. If she makes a complaint about something we could lose our jobs. Or worse, our place. Better safe than sorry."

"Fine. When we go in you can come with me."

He hadn't taken anything, the complaint was bogus, but she was right. He hadn't covered his ass and it was his word against a disgruntled tenant's. He didn't worry about shit like this in the army—there, integrity and reputation had meaning. Out here among the civvies there was no honor. At least none that he could see.

They turned the corner, a few hundred yards from their own unit. Approaching them was another tenant walking her dog. She rented the unit downstairs from theirs. She smiled as they passed and the two returned the greeting. The woman barely spoke a word of English; a smile was all that was required. At the end of a nylon red leash was a yappy Scottish terrier. When they passed the dog stopped, turned, and barked at them. Satisfied it had made its point, it ambled along the walk.

Neither Dan nor Heather bothered to look back.

————

Wednesday

Both were expecting the worst after Hollander Rice, Holly to his friends, started complaining about the smell. He called them that morning and they came right over. Holly's unit was directly below the tenant whose apartment they had been trying to inspect.

"There's something going bad upstairs," Holly told them. "It stinks, and there's noises."

Dan lifted his chin and sniffed the air. There was an odor of something.

"What kind of noises?" Heather asked.

Holly rubbed his nose, focused on the ceiling and said, "I don't know, critter-like I guess. I hear them scuttling across the floor late at night."

"Them," Dan puzzled. "Holly what are you driving at?"

"I don't know, Dan, maybe she has rodents. These people have different standards of living than the rest of us. You know what I mean."

Dan ignored the 'these people' remark. He couldn't get wrapped up in that, it was politically incorrect. If he started slinging around words he might be thinking, the corporation would toss him and Heather out their collective ear. "Have you seen any rodents in your unit, Holly?"

"No, but there's definitely something going on up there." He was rubbing his nose and Heather wondered if he was itching for them to leave so he could jam a digit in there and dig out whatever it was that was bothering him. He pinched his nostrils between his index finger and thumb so hard the skin turned pink, making him look like a cartoonish drunk. Realizing Heather was watching, he removed his hand. "I've got allergies and right now they're driving me nuts."

"Allergies to what?" Heather asked.

"Oh you name it. Dogs, cats, pollen, ragweed. If I get stung by a bee I'm a goner."

"Wow, Holly, you need to be careful," Heather said, trying very hard not to sound patronizing.

Dan wasn't thinking about Holly's allergies; he was thinking about the tenant upstairs. The tenant was Romani, which Dan first thought to be Romanian, but Heather looked it up on the web and said, "She's a gypsy. Listen to this. 'Romani first originated in Asia and immigrated to Europe and then to the Americas.' This is kind of cool. A real gypsy living here."

He really didn't care if she was from the North Pole. She was just one in a long line of people who were accommodated while others were ignored. Her name was Nicolita Bashen, and until Dan actually heard her speak he thought she might be from South East Asia, maybe India or Pakistan. But her accent was closer to Spanish, so then he thought Mexican. But on that he was also wrong.

He first met her when she was accompanied by Murray Kipman to view the place. She was a pretty lady in her early thirties, copper skin, raven hair, very easy on the eyes. Murray was the tenant counsellor who handled the subsidized portfolios, or as Dan referred to it: The Freeloader File. The freeloaders were tenants who got government subsidy on their rent. A one bedroom normally retailed at $900.00 a month, but the freeloaders only paid based upon income and family circumstance. In her case she was only paying $210.00 a month and the government— or rather the taxpayer—was picking up the remaining $690.00. Another tenant who'd emigrated from Iran with his wife and four kids was only paying $110.00 on a $1300.00 five-bedroom unit. He claimed to be living on his social assistance and child benefit checks. Meanwhile, the guy was selling Persian Rugs out of his basement. Every now and again a high end car, be it Caddy, Lincoln, or the odd Lexus or Beamer, would show up. Dan speculated that was when the money exchanged hands, because not long after a dumpy old blue ford pickup, driven by one of the tenant's friends or cousins, would arrive to pick up one of the rugs.

Imagine that. He even delivered. Dan never saw the rugs arrive, he only saw them leaving, which left him to wonder if the inventory came under the cover of darkness. Or through a tunnel that went directly to Iran.

Cheating Fuckers!

The whole system pissed Dan off. He and Heather had only come here because his career in the military had been cut short after he blew out his knee. Eleven years of service, not a fucking blemish, and they gave him the big kiss off. Sure, he got a partial pension, but it wasn't enough to live on. They applied for subsidized housing, but were rejected—apparently, his pension tipped him just above the line. So the only thing they could do was apply for the superintendent position. Heather didn't want to do it, but they needed a cash break until Dan figured out what he was going to do with the rest of his life. Now six months into the job, Dan still had no idea what to do with himself and his moods were often dark, brooding, even resentful.

"All right, thanks Holly, we'll look into it." He turned to go.

"When," Holly asked.

Dan turned back, then thoughtfully looked to Heather. "We have to get clearance. I'll give her another call and try and set something up. If she dodges me this time, we'll go in with the master key."

Heather gave him a look of approval.

"I'll let Murray know about the stink. He might want to call you for confirmation."

"Uh, okay." Holly suddenly looked concerned. "This will be anonymous right?"

"No worries, Holly, it will be confidential."

———

Thursday

"At the tone please leave a message," said the automated recording.

"Hello, Miss Bashen, this Dan the superintendent. I have been trying to reschedule a meeting with you for the better part of a week. As it stands now, I have tried three times to set up a viewing of your unit and have not been able to do so." He tightened his grip on the receiver and took a measured breath. "You are my last inspection and I don't mind saying that I'm getting a little frustrated. I am now waiting for a call from your tenant counsellor, Murray Kipman. If you don't contact me by the time Mr. Kipman calls, I am going to get authorization to enter your unit with or without your permission. I'd prefer you were there. Call me, Miss Bashen." He hung the receiver back in its cradle and looked to Heather.

"Maybe she split," Heather said. They'd had a few two tenants abandon their units since assuming the superintendent position. In both cases, the units were a muddle of furniture, unwashed dishes, and filthy floors. Heather had come to realize that some people were absolute pigs.

61

"Yeah, maybe." Dan pushed past her into the kitchen and poured himself a fresh coffee. "What do you think it is that Holly was talking about? The stink I mean."

"I don't know, Dan. The place is probably a disaster."

"Marvellous. If it's that bad they can spring for a cleaner. A hundred bucks isn't worth cleaning up someone else's filth." He sipped the coffee. It was bitter, like his mood.

That afternoon, Murray finally called and listened patiently as Dan outlined their dilemma. Dan tried not to sound overzealous, but there was still urgency in his tone. The work didn't end at the inspections; there was always something when you oversaw a townhouse complex of this size.

"I need to get these inspections wrapped up, Murray. I have units to paint, bathrooms that need new caulk, electrical work. She's holding us up."

"How many times have you tried to set up an appointment?"

Dan became irritated by the question. *Fucking pencil pusher, way to support your people.* "Three times. Three times Heather and I have set up and three times she dodged us."

Murray inhaled and then exhaled. "I'm just covering all the bases, Dan. The tenant act is a tricky piece of business and I don't mind telling you that in a lot of cases they are a very biased bunch. We go barging in without dotting all the 'i's' and crossing all the 't's'…Well, you get the jest."

Dan got the gist all right. The whole show was being run by a bunch of lawyers who were more interested in covering the asses of their investors. Gutless pencil pushers just like Murray Kipman, well… They were part of the problem; that was the gist. Rather than speak his mind, he asked, "What would suggest then?"

"I'd suggest that we try and set up a meeting. If she is present when you are there, it lowers the liability on our part. I'd also suggest you don't go in alone for obvious reasons."

Dan's face fell, an ugly scowl tugging at his mouth. Anger bubbled up from his guts, turning his voice into a growl. "What obvious reasons?"

Murray sighed. "Sexual harassment, theft, verbal abuse. The list is endless, Dan."

He relaxed a little. "Okay. How about this? The tenant downstairs can give us a shout when he hears something and we'll go over with the master key. I'll take Heather and we'll announce ourselves when we arrive. Will that work?"

Murray said nothing, simply breathing in and out considering the proposal. "Three times, Dan?"

"Three times," Dan replied. His patience exhausted. "Come on, Murray, it's not like we're being unreasonable."

"Okay, talk to your tenant downstairs. Is that Mr. Rice?"

"Yeah, Holly. He's says there's a smell."

"If Mr. Rice says she's home, you and Heather go over. Make sure she knows you're coming in. Be extra loud if you have to."

"I will."

———

Friday, mid-morning

The call from Holly came a little after 9 a.m. He said there were 'sounds' upstairs, like someone was moving around, but he didn't know for how long. He again asked for discretion in the matter and, of course, Dan gave him another assurance.

Using a closed fist, he rapped hard on the door.

There was no response.

After a second he did it again, giving Heather a solemn look, then he reached into his pocket and produced the townhouse key ring. "I just know that this is going to be a treat," he mumbled, flipping the keys over, trying to find the master.

"I thought Holly said she was home?"

"He did." Dan smirked and lowered his voice. "She's probably hiding in a closet up there."

Heather was uneasy and didn't like the idea of confronting this woman without warning, but Dan was right. They had given her ample time to set up an appointment and she kept dodging them.

He inserted the key into the lock and turned. It clicked, he turned the knob, pushed the door open, and stepped over the threshold. "Miss Bashen! Hello? It's Dan the super!"

"Oh my god," Heather said bringing a hand up to her mouth.

The aroma was dreadful, a sour putrid fragrance, rotten meat or garbage intermingled with something else neither could put their fingers on. The foyer was a clutter of newspapers and the carpeted stairs leading up to the unit were stained with God-knew-what. To the left of the doorway, a half full black garbage bag lay deflated and lucent with moisture. He clutched the jamb and turned back to Heather ready to proclaim, 'I told you so.' But before he could step up onto his soapbox, something skittered down his arm. He drew it back defensively and he let out a shrill, "What the fuck!"

Cockroaches!

He batted them away, bolting out of the doorway, almost knocking Heather over in the process. The almond-shaped bugs, all four of them, tumbled onto the ground, two of the four scuttling off in different directions, seeking cover. The other two weren't as lucky. Dan brought a foot down. Their shells crunched beneath his sneaker.

They looked at each other, then back into the doorway. Dozens of cockroaches were congregating in the corners, huddling beneath the open garbage bag, peering out at them. Dan stuck his head back into the doorway and peered up at the trim above the door, then pulled back. They stymied along and over the walls. They must have dropped down on him.

Like airborne para-jumpers free falling from the trim when I opened the door.

"Shit!"

"What?" Heather blurted.

"They're everywhere! Bugs, I hate fucking bugs!"

Heather laughed nervous teenage-like titters. "Scared?"

Dan smiled back. "No. Well…"

It was a nice smile, a return to normality, before they—the Army—stole her husband away and replaced him with the dark sulky man who was mad at everyone and everything. That smile was sweet and caring, the old Dan.

"Are you?" He was still grinning, his eyes darting between her and the open doorway.

She giggled the same way a girl might before entering a Funhouse. "Nooo!"

"Sure." He reached out and took her hand, feeling the connection. She looked pretty standing out here, her smile pushing against her cheekbones, accentuating those big blue eyes that reminded him of a young Goldie Hawn. He thought about when they first met, how he was sure she was out of his league.

Her hair had been longer then, the shade of blonde a tad dirtier, but Heather was still a looker. The men who lived here turned their heads when she walked by. These days Dan seemed not to notice, blind inside a self-imposed purgatory of indifference. But he was noticing now. There had been many ups and down during their fifteen-year relationship and it seemed that weird little moments like this drew them back together.

"Well, let's get this over with shall we."

"What if she's up there?"

"Well then, I guess she gets a big surprise. We gave her lots of warning, hon." He took her hand and they entered the foyer. Dan bolted under the doorway tugging Heather along, trying to avoid another stick of cockroach para-jumpers. He yanked the door closed and a fresh batch of the bugs spilled onto the floor, scattering left and right. "We're definitely going to need an exterminator."

"It smells horrible." Heather gagged in a half whisper. She couldn't connect this pigpen with Nicolita Bashen. She didn't seem like a dirty person. She was always neatly dressed, her make-up done, hair taken care of, and she was pretty. Pretty enough to catch Dan's eye. She'd caught him taking inventory of that slender body on more than one occasion. And of course this set off a spark of jealousy, but not enough to ignite an outburst. She wouldn't air such insecurity—doing that might damage their already fragile relationship.

Mounting upward was a stairwell covered with low crushed gray carpet. Gray was an easy color to hide stains like animal shit, coffee, or even blood. Dan and Heather had had a tenant whose dog was not fixed and when it went into heat it bled. The tenant was evicted for not paying his rent. When he vacated he left the place in a real state. Dime- sized droplets of copper marked every room in the place. The tenant had purposelessly walked his bleeding dog around the unit, leaving no surface unmarked. Along with the dime-sized marks came a copper bouquet not unlike raw liver; this place smelled like that. Sour, malignant.

Dan squeezed Heather's hand. "You ready?"

She nodded, one hand covering her mouth.

At their feet tiny eyes watched.

There were fourteen stairs leading to a landing that cut left down a short hallway. What lay beyond, a living room, an eat-in kitchen, a bathroom and a single bedroom. As Dan led her up the stairwell, he took each step with great care. The stairs were steep and though there was a handrail, neither he nor Heather wanted to touch it. The plastic coated railing was covered in roach droppings. Dan was wishing now that he'd put on a set of latex gloves, but it was too late to go back. A third of the way up, Heather gagged and almost dry heaved. The aroma was intensifying. It reminded him of how a defrosting freezer smelled. Heather pulled the neck of her shirt up over her mouth and this made Dan laugh.

"We're not going to rob a bank there, Toots."

She pulled it down, sneered at him, and then pulled it back up.

Dan was thinking that they'd have to strip right down and get into the shower when this was over. He didn't want to drag any roach eggs back to their own unit. He made a mental note to go to the utility shed and get a garbage bag. As gross as this was, he thought he might try and talk Heather into a little shower sex once the inspection was over. Climbing the last few steps he noted that the dark splotches in carpet were larger up here. And there was something else.

No roaches. Why? Wouldn't there be more food up there?

"Miss Bashen, are you there? It's Dan the super. I have my wife Heather with me. Are you there?" He took a final step up onto the landing, Heather in tow, and turned to face the living room. Then he froze, his grip on Heather's hand clamping down like a vice. She pulled her hand free just as his other hand clamped over her mouth.

She tried to pull back and he brought his other hand up, drawing his index fingers across his lips to signify the universal sign of hush. Except Dan wasn't thinking Hush. He was thinking, oh my sweet Jesus and Heather shut your mouth! And there was something else. Spiders!

Dan hated spiders. Even worse than roaches.

The living room was upholstered in a layer of web that rose in drifts at left and right angles. The sofa, the largest piece of furniture, was anchored on every corner. Silk funnels large enough to insert a hand swirled inward at those anchor points, leaving Dan to consider morosely how big the occupants of those whirlpools of silk were. He could only guess, but he wasn't waiting around to find out.

We're going to need an army of exterminators, he thought madly.

"Back up. Back up," he whispered. "We gotta get out of here." Heather didn't just back up, she was tugging him down the stairs, her eyes wide. She didn't need to be told. Farther inside the unit, in another room there was a sound, a soft bump, then a scuttling sound. Something had heard them. And it was coming closer!

"Come on let's go," Dan cried all at once and they bounded down the stairs comically, taking two and three steps at a time.

Dan's heart was a jackhammer, thudding against his chest cavity, reverberating in his ears. He hardly noticed the cockroaches raining down on him as he fumbled the door open; he was too busy pushing Heather through the door, wanting her to hurry up and get out of the way. When he got through, he slammed it behind him, causing the single rectangular pane inside it to rattle.

Heather was pulling at her top, shaking the cockroaches out. "Yuck! Oh yuck!"

Dan felt one of the little bugger's scamper across

the back of his neck and he reached under his shirt collar, hooking his middle finger to dig it out. It burrowed away and rather than flick it out he squashed it against his bare skin. Normally, that would have driven him nuts, but he was focused on the front door. Absently, he flicked three more off of his clothing as he approached the glass pane. He peered in and up the stairs, trying to see if what they heard had come to meet them. The angle wasn't right so he knelt down. He could see the landing, but it was empty except for a thin ray of daylight that was coming from the living room. He cupped his hands around his eyes and, for a second, he thought there was an interruption in that light.

Where is it? Where is it? Something clinched his shoulder then.

His scream was bloodcurdling.

Oh my god! Spider! Spider!

The thing he had felt on his shoulder was not a spider, but Heather's assuring hand. She was just about to ask what he was looking at when he uncoiled from his kneeling position, screaming and batting at her hand. He was still screaming, tearing at his shirt, eyes darting madly backward in his sockets.

Heather screamed as well, but only because Dan had scared her.

———

Friday—Afternoon

"Unbelievable," he cussed.

One thing Dan hated about civvies was their apparent lack of dedication when it came to Friday afternoons. Murray Kipman was gone for the day and it wasn't even 2 p.m. Now, sitting by the phone it seemed he had a decision to make. Without Murray to give authorization, he had to get an exterminator into that place, but making such a call without authorization would ruffle a few feathers. Ruffle a few 'Bean Counters' was more like it.

He left a quick message. "Murray, this is Dan. I've got a cockroach infestation of epic proportion. I'm going to call Mountain Exterminators. The tenant is Nicolita Bashen. Unit 46. Call me when you get this." He thought about mentioning the spider webs, but decided to leave that for later; after the exterminator had gone through the place.

"They aren't going to be very happy about this," Heather said.

"Tough shit. I'm making a command decision. Those bugs start moving they'll infest the whole building. Besides, it's not my fault the corporation is too cheap to have weekend staffing. I just hope someone from Mountain is available today."

And has someone who knows how to deal with spiders, he thought.

He hadn't actually seen any spiders, just their handiwork. Webs hanging over all the furniture like silken tapestry and the funnels at the corners of the sofa. And there had been that noise.

What had Holly said? Scuttling. Yes, that word seemed quite appropriate.

Dan felt his skin crawl. Fucking spiders!

He made the call.

Two hours later, Dan was met by a nondescript van at the front of the Bashen unit and out stepped a tall, thin man with a frizzy tangle of gray wearing blue coveralls. On the left breast, just above the pocket, an embroidered name tag read: Jim.

"Boy, you got your work cut out for you."

"Uh huh." Jim, apparently having seen and done it all, cast a doubtful glance Dan's way, and then he pulled out something that looked like a prop from Star Trek. It was chrome and looked sort of like a futuristic gun. The tip looked like the end of a piping bag used for decorating cakes. "Okay, show me where the bugs are."

"What is that?"

"It's called a paste gun. You got roaches, right? Well this is roach paste."

Dan smiled. "Is that all you've got?"

Jim didn't seem in the joking mood. "Look, I'm missing my supper and the hockey game. Show me the bugs and I'll take care of it."

This guy thought he was overreacting. Probably got

calls like this all the time. Two roaches were probably an infestation to the average caller, but this wasn't average.

"There's a major infestation in this unit, and not only roaches. There's spider web all over the upstairs. I don't think your little paste gun is going to cut it?"

"What's your name?"

"Dan."

"Okay, Dan, here's the thing. I deal with this stuff every day. I need to take a look. For now, I'll go in armed with my roach paste. If I need something bigger, say like my fogger, I'll come back and get it, but I'm not unloading all my gear until I've had a look."

"Suit yourself."

They proceeded to the front door and Dan unlocked it.

"Anybody home?"

"No, but just in case." Dan leaned in. "Miss Bashen. It's Dan the super. I'm back with an exterminator."

They waited.

No answer.

Jim the Exterminator was looking at the roaches scurrying around at the front door. "She's got nests."

"What?"

"Roaches are nocturnal. They only come out in the

open when they're overpopulated. Your tenant has got a nest somewhere."

"I'm more worried about the spiders."

"Did you see any?"

"No, but I…" He wanted to say heard, but knew how ridiculous that sounded. "I saw a lot of web upstairs."

"Cycle of life. Spiders appear to eat the roaches, probably not before long the centipedes show up to eat the spiders." Jim the Exterminator stepped through the door. Halfway in he stopped and looked back at Dan. "You coming up?"

"I'll stay here if you don't mind."

"Not at all." He stepped into the foyer, took a cursory glance around and said, "I'll definitely be coming back for my fogger." Then he started up the stairs.

Dan watched him go, feeling guilty for not being more forceful in his warning. He thought of the noise he'd heard, that light thumping on the carpet, and it conjured up all sorts of nightmarish ideas. The very thought was ludicrous. Spiders didn't make noise when they marched across carpet or floor. They were silent stalkers. That was one of the things that made them so damned scary. One minute there's nothing, and then the eight- legged hairy creature is moving at high speed, unafraid. He moved away from the doorway, back down the steps and onto the walk. His arms were a mass of goose pimples, the hairs on his neck and arms stood erect.

Exterminator Jim had only been gone for five minutes, but to Dan it felt like fifty. He shifted his weight between his left and right foot, approached the door then backed off. He quietly scolded himself. What kind of soldier were you if a few bugs have got you rattled? You should have gone in there with him.

As Dan waited for Jim to reappear—considering entering the unit and redeeming his manhood—Heather heard the doorbell ring. She descended the stairwell to see a silhouette through the frosted glass in her front door. She pulled the door open. Nicolita Bashen stood before her. The two women were about the same height, and almost nose to nose.

"Miss Bashen?"

"May I come in?" She looked dismayed, but unthreatening.

"Dan is over at your place with the exterminator." She widened the crack in the door.

"Yes, I know, he sent me over." She took a step forward.

"Oh?" Heather opened the door. "Please come in."

———

Back at the unit, Dan finally steeled himself to enter. His right foot hovered over the threshold when Jim appeared at the top of the stairs. The exterminator had a strange look on his face. He reached out and clutched the hand rail, took one step down, and then dragged his other leg behind him.

What the hell's the matter with him?

"Jim?" Dan stepped inside, cockroaches crunching beneath his feet. "You okay?"

Jim turned his head slightly left and Dan saw it. Two dark fingers, then three, then four and he realized what it was. The exterminator took another step. Even from this distance and angle he could see that Jim's face hung on one side like a man who had suffered a stroke. "Kid, close the door." Drool spilled from his lip.

Two of the dark fingers lifted up from Jim's cheek, dancing slightly in the air, then came down and Jim moaned while trying to take another step and fell against the rail. The spider was the size of Dan's hand.

My god! He's paralyzed!

Dan took a step back. More crunches sounded beneath his feet.

Then he heard it, a cacophony of thumps, like a litter of kittens all bounding from high places when the dinner bell was rung. Except it wasn't kittens and it, rather they, were coming!

Jim moaned and began to slide down the rail. As he did, the spider clamped tighter, deepening its bite and, as a result, his legs became elastic. Tumbling forward, he spat out a final slurred warning. "They're coming! Run!"

He fell forward onto the stairwell, sliding down the carpet, each stair bumping against his sternum. Two of his ribs cracked on the way down and his other cheek, the one that didn't have a hand-sized spider affixed to it, rubbed raw against the carpet. The spider riding the old guy's face looked like a hairy eight-legged surfer.

Dan stepped forward, intent on helping Jim, when they appeared, and the courage he'd been assembling ran out of him, along with contents of his bladder. It was his intention to squash the big bug using his boot if necessary and pull Jim clear, but that all changed when the others appeared. What happened next occurred in a matter of seconds, but in Dan's mind it was long, drawn out, and surreal. As Jim bumped down the steps, his head buckled under from the drag of the carpeting. His right arm was twisted sickly, which indicated that it had broken in the fall. The face-hugging spider was almost a blur, but its two front legs waved momentarily and then it struck down again, biting into the already yellowing skin on Jim's face. He was three steps from the foyer when the others appeared. They lined the edge of the landing. First one, then two, then four, then six and eight and…

Dan stopped counting because it was only a fleeting pause. Long enough for each of the spiders to take in the sound which had roused them. Then, collectively, they came down the stairs. One jumped on the railing, ascending and closing half the distance before Jim had even hit the main foyer. Two others sprung up onto the walls, crawling downward with the same unstoppable momentum. The remaining hairy bastards thumped down the stairs. Dan took another step and this time there was no more crunching. Apparently the cockroaches knew when to get the hell out of Dodge.

In the last two seconds, an inevitable a scenario played out in Dan's mind in which he reached out and grabbed Jim's busted arm and, in a single heave, he yanked the old guy through the doorway. Simultaneously, he brought his elbow down on the surfer spider and crushed it into Jim's cheek with a splat that caused a gush of sickening yellow mucous. Before he could get up and close the door, he felt a light thud against his shoulder, then his back and then his head.

They were going to bite! They were going to kill him!

And it was in that fleeting premonition that Dan stepped back over the threshold and slammed the door shut, sealing the exterminator in as the creeping death descended upon him. He watched in horror as they pounced, digging in, biting, and with each poisonous sting Jim's body convulsed. Dan looked on horrified, but he could not tear his eyes away. Shame would come later. Two of the arachnids, unsatisfied with the meal at hand, sprung at Dan, bouncing off the glass. Persistently, they thumped against it, again and again and again. They were trapped and for that Dan was thankful, although he would never forgive himself for leaving Jim the Exterminator to such a horrific fate.

———

Holly was the one who called the police. They arrived on the scene expecting a domestic dispute, only to find a horrific sight that would turn out to be one of the most bizarre crime scenes ever recorded. Upon their arrival, they found Dan shivering on the stairwell, Heather at his side, her arm wrapped protectively around him. The allergenic Hollander Rice met them at the sidewalk and filled them in.

The police took in the spectacle that was Jim, now being cocooned by his killers right before their eyes. A call was put in and another exterminator arrived on the scene, but this fellow had something bigger than a paste gun. Looking like a Ghostbuster—armed with a wand and a tank of deadly poison strapped to his back, and accompanied by officers with weapons drawn—he entered the unit and exterminated every living creature in the foyer. Even the hiding cockroaches met their end. With that done, they climbed the stairs, but instead of finding more spiders they instead found five more bodies, all cocooned, and in various states of decay. Homicide detectives were dispatched to the scene.

As they went through the place, Detective Bob Halsey remarked to his partner, "Where are they?"

"Who? The spiders," his partner Hugh Ogden asked. "Exterminator killed em."

"No. Where are the aquariums?"

"Maybe she kept them as pets. Let them run around."

Halsey sniffed. "How the fuck are we going to write this up, Oggy? What the fuck was the deal here?"

"The woman was a predator. Some use poison. Some use a gun. A knife. This one used spiders."

"You do know how crazy that sounds?"

Ogden did and said. "Shithouse rat crazy, Bob, but lacking a better explanation it's sure how it looks."

In the months that followed it was discovered that the spiders were a deadly species whose scientific name was: Phoneutria, better known in South America as the Wandering Spider. This particular species was native to Brazil and considered to be one of the deadliest on Earth. Detectives Halsey and Ogden traced Nicolita Bashen back to her Romani roots in Brazil. They could only speculate that she had been luring men to her apartment and using the spiders to kill them. This act began only a week after she got the keys to the unit. The oldest victim, a man in his forties found in the bedroom, had been there for over five months. The spiders had drained him dry, leaving only a web- draped, mummified corpse. The bizarre aspects of the story were sealed and kept out of the papers. As for Nicolita Bashen, the only named person of interest, she was never found.

———

Heather never spoke of her encounter with Nicolita Bashen. She did not mention the visit to the police on the day she was interviewed because she'd been smoking a bit of weed that afternoon. This was something she did to cope with the stress of living with Dan's erratic mood swings. It was her secret. Even Dan didn't know. She was getting the grass from one of their tenants. When Nicolita Bashen stepped through her doorway, it didn't seem real, Heather wondered if the weed was spiked with something, an opiate of some sort.

As her husband called to Jim the Exterminator, Nicolita Bashen closed the door behind her and reached back, clicking the deadbolt over.

"What are you doing," Heather asked.

"I wasn't finished," Nicolita told her. "They are my children. I needed two more days. Two more men, but now it will all be ruined. The cycle will have to be restarted."

"I don't understand," Heather said and thought, Is this a dream?

"You," Nicolita spat, both hands reaching up, taking Heather's cheeks in each. She tried to pull back, lower her head and look away, but could not. Nicolita's grip tightened on each cheek, but worse her hands had begun to morph. The appendages, once fingers, became hard and prickly legs that dug in with tiny backward barbs. The arachnid legs massaged each cheek as the fangs on each creature salivated. Nicolita spoke, but her lips remained pursed.

"We are of the Romani Phoneutria. Wanderers and protectors of the detlene poko who walk the jungle floors by night."

"Please let go of me," Heather whimpered.

Nicolita's jaw unhinged like a snake, the skin on her face retracting, turning cold gray. Her gaping mouth widened into a dark cavernous burrow. In the back of her throat her uvula hung bloated, pulsing, but it was not that. No, not a punching bag hanging between the tonsils, but a bloated egg sac waiting to deliver its clutch. Behind the sac, eight dark eyes peered back that could only belong to a...

You will find nourishment for Detline.

The spider emerged, clipping the egg sac and wrapping it protectively.

Heather's eyes widened in horror. "Oh, dear God, no."

"You will be surrogate to the spirits of dead children."

The arachnid snipped, then pushed that sac forward, rolling it across Nicolita's tongue.

Suddenly she was pulling her in toward the advancing spider.

"No, no, no..."

Nicolita Bashen pulled Heather into an open mouth kiss, her tongue delivering the sac of offspring.

There was a momentary gag.

"The children of Romani Phoneutria," Nicolita said and receded.

Then there was only darkness.

She had no concept of how long she'd been out. Her throat felt dry and tickled. There was no sign of Nicolita and the dream, if was a dream, was beginning to fade. Heather stumbled up the stairwell and went into the bathroom. There, she mustered her courage before opening her mouth wide and, after a moment, she laughed nervously, thinking herself stupid.

"No more chronic for this girl," she told the reflection staring back at her.

After brushing her teeth and spraying a bit of perfume on her clothes, she exited the apartment and a minute later she found her husband on his knees in front of Nicolita Bashen's unit. She peered through the rectangular glass and saw the horror. She reached for her cell phone, but it was still on the kitchen table.

"Stay here Dan," she said, panicked, then ran up and pounded on Holly's door.

"Heather," Holly said as he opened his unit door.

"Call the police, Holly! Call the police!"

———

Eight Months Later

Dan and Heather left the superintendent position and moved on. Dan spent some months in treatment for post-traumatic stress disorder. The irony that he was being treated for a disorder that often affected soldiers but was due to his civilian job as a superintendent was not lost on him. Three months later, he realized that he would never get over the events of that day. He could only come to terms with the horror and with that he decided it was time to get on with living and try and leave the past behind.

He dusted off his resume, took a couple of courses to supplement his military training, and applied for a position as an explosives technician at a diamond mine in the Northwest Territories. After an intensive four stage interview process, his application was accepted and he was hired on. The new job paid well; Dan would fly in for three weeks and then be home for two. He finally felt he was coming out the other side and the job fit well with his previous lifestyle.

They were at the airport; he was about to fly in on his first rotation. He felt giddy and nervous.

"What kind of name is Acadia," Heather asked of her husband's new employer.

"They're a French company," Dan said and smiled. "I love you, Heather."

"I love you, too, Dan."

"Thank you for putting up with my bullshit."

She smiled. "You better get your ass through security."

He kissed and embraced her. "I'll see you in three

weeks."

"Three weeks," she agreed.

He picked up his carry-on bag and got into the security line up. She stood there and waited until he disappeared behind the frosted glass. Then she walked back out to the car and got in. She adjusted the rear view mirror. Three weeks and he would be back.

Would that be enough time?

She opened her mouth. The egg sac had broken last night, the spiderlings retreating down her esophagus, hiding in the darkness and waiting to be fed. They were the 'Detline' a word she did not understand when it was spoken by Nicolita, but now she understood. They were the spirits of dead children, the children of Romani Phoneutria, and they were hungry.

Tonight the feeding would begin.

———

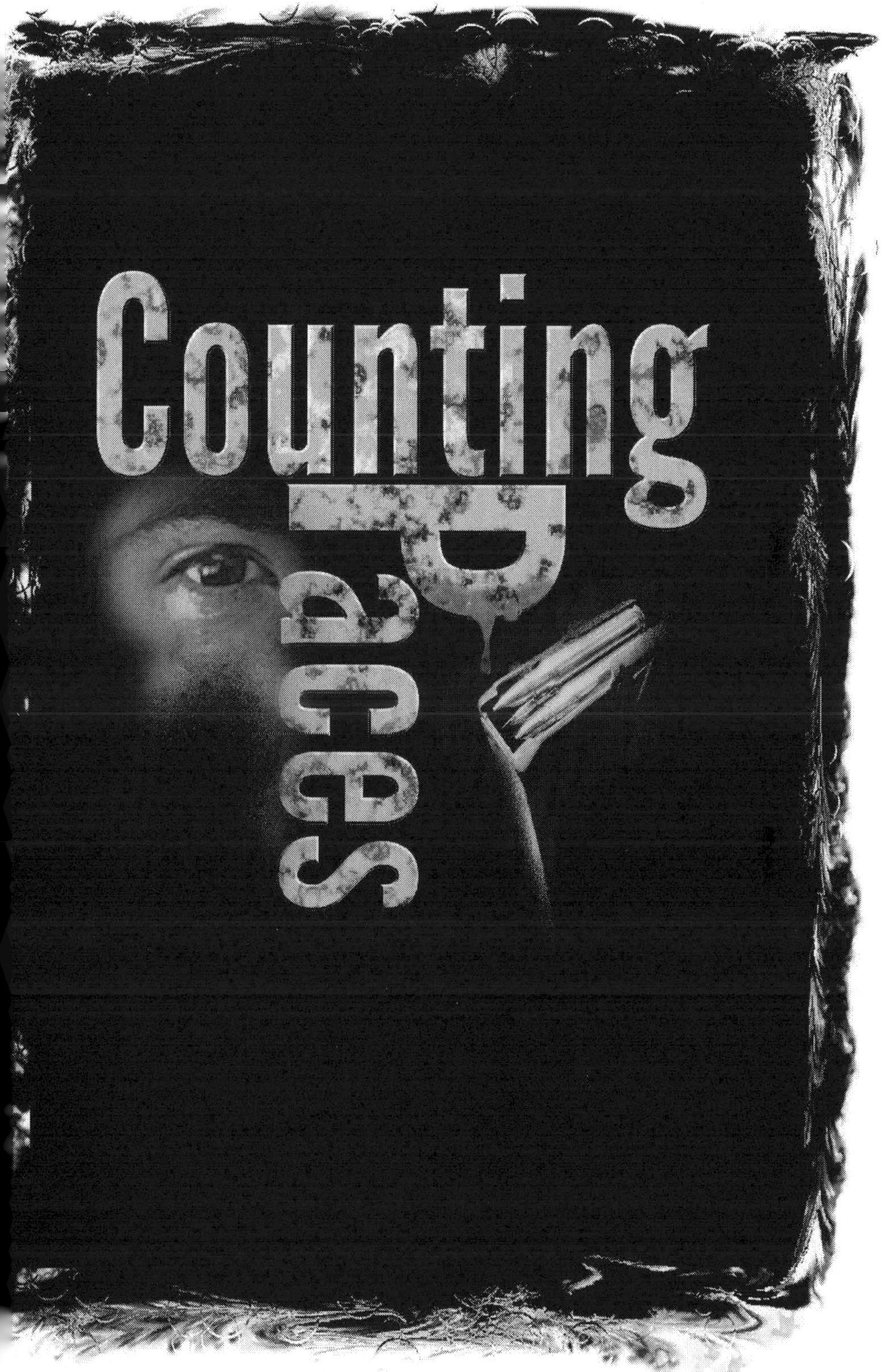
Counting
Days

Counting Paces

Sarah was still in bed when I started the car and warmed it up for two minutes. This was something she insisted upon. The car was hers, a present from her father when we married. Along with the car, he'd given me sound mechanical advice. "Always warm it up. It gives the engine a chance to self-lubricate, Michael. Two minutes before you put it under load will add years to the life of the engine." I don't know if this was true or not, but it didn't really matter. Sarah thought it was.

I sat patiently smoking a cigarette, watching the digital clock on the stereo as time dragged out. The readout flipped from 7:05 over to 7:06 am, but I didn't dare pull out of that driveway until exactly two minutes were up. She might have been in bed, but she would know.

Two minutes and thirty seconds later, the little base bungalow, along with Sarah, were in my rear view mirror. I drove carefully—not wanting to scuff my boots. We'd been living on the Army Base for a little over a year now. My supervisor, Sergeant Pierce, doesn't like me much. He's always on my case about my boots not being shiny enough, and of course there's the creases in both my uniform pants and dress shirts—they aren't sharp enough. I work in a Motor Transport with 8 other soldiers. We are the misfits, sent over because we didn't quite fit in with our combat units. Some of us have discipline problems— some don't work well with their peers—others are just plain stupid. That's why we're here, or at least that's what Pierce thinks, or so he told Master Corporal Crabbe over a cigarette. He calls us, "problem children".

Pierce is a real ball buster. After the last inspection, I ended up doing four weekends of extra duties because he couldn't see his crooked smile in the toes of my boots. This oversight on my part led to a serious dressing down. I'd like to say in front of, but I was really amongst a robotic audience of soldiers staring into the abyss and waiting for their own turn of abuse.

"What's the matter with you, Hicks," he yelled at me. "This is basic fucking training stuff, what the fuck is your problem! Are you simple, or is it you just don't give a shit!"

He wasn't asking me for an answer, he was stating his opinion. So I stood there at the chow, while he went up one side of me and down the other. I stared into a blurred chasm of unfocused anxiety. I didn't want to say anything. Replying would only make it worse, whatever excuse I gave would not be good enough. But inside my head? I was screaming at the fucker, screaming at the top of my lungs.

I arrived at the parking lot outside the compound and looked at the building I worked in, while taking in the distance I would have to walk from my parking spot to the building. I locked Sarah's precious car, and then I began counting paces.

1 2 3 4 5 6 7……. And so it went.

As I counted the paces from the gravel parking lot, the hours of work I'd put into my boots the night before were being eroded by the fine granules of dirt kicked up as I walked on. It worked like an abrasive on the spit shine, dulling it with every step. If not for the count, I would be forced to listen to the corrosive sound inside my head.

I continued counting, the words barely passing my lips.

47... 48... 49…

The counting soothes me, keeps me from breaking into rage at the stupidity of it all. Here they want us turned out in our best bib and tucker and they make us park our personal vehicles in a dust bowl parking lot almost a km from the building. Motherfuckers!

122…123... 124…

I've been doing it every day for the last eight months and it calms me. Gets me ready to face Pierce and keeps me from going completely off the rails. Outwardly, I look like any other fuck-up in this motley crew, but inside I'm like a pressure cooker. As I walked I heard a call behind me.

"Hicks! Hey Hicks!" It was Randall, just getting out of his own car, I ignored him, keeping the count in my head.

Somehow, I'd lost time and found myself at the main building. The count had ended, 775 paces, and I began to smile. I thought it would have topped 800 that time. Over the last eight months the paces alternated by about ten, between 769 and 779, but never over. Over 800 would mean something, especially if I have no hand in it.

I stopped at the doorway, the count was over.

778 paces.

Didn't make it this time.

I took a deep breath and entered the MT. As I walked in, I could see the guys milling about and joking. Randall stepped through the doorway behind me. "Hey Hicks, didn't you hear me?"

I turned and smiled. "Sorry Randall, I was daydreaming, I guess."

"No sweat." He glanced down at my parade boots. "Wow, your boots look good."

"Thanks," I pulled a kiwi cloth out of my pocket and carefully wiped the dust from them, ever weary of leaving a mark or a scratch.

"Fall in." MCpl Crabbe called out. The troop got into formation, waiting for Pierce to do roll call. It was always a crap shoot whether or not he'd do an inspection. "Attention." Crabbe barked in a drill voice that just didn't measure up.

I tried not to smile, but did anyway.

Then Pierce marched out, tearing the smile from my face and setting a storm of anxiety loose in my stomach. He wasn't even in position when he gave the order. "Open order march!"

Guess the fucker is going to inspect us today, I thought.

We opened ranks.

"Right dress!"

All of us except the last man on the right brought their arms up—cocking their heads right—then spreading out and aligning ourselves into three uniform ranks. I was dead center in the second rank.

"Eyes front!"

With precision, we cut our arms to our sides while our heads and eyes snapped front. Normally in a situation like this a sergeant will stand the two rear ranks at ease, but not Pierce, he kept us all at attention. I fucking hated him for this!

As he made his way through the first rank he berated soldiers for their boots, their rank insignia, their mustaches and their haircuts. I waited for him to swing around and give me the once over, holding myself firm and remembering how he had torn me a new asshole in front of my peers. I remembered feeling so little in front of him—remembered him shouting at me, asking me what was the matter with me, was I stupid or just lazy.

I just stood there and took it, but I wanted to scream back at him. I wanted to tell him that shining my boots wasn't high on my priority list. Wanted to tell him I had bigger things on my mind.

"Why can't you find time to put some effort into your boots!"

I wanted to look him right in the eye and shriek, "Shining my boots hasn't been at the top of my priority list Sarge! Would it be on top of your priority list if you thought your wife was fucking someone else?" But I said nothing, and for my sins I received four weekend duties. Four days for Sarah to roll around with whomever it was she was fucking while I was paying for a Sergeant Pierce inspection.

Pierce walked behind the first rank, checking their haircuts. When he got to the end and started on the second rank my heart sped up, my knees trembled and I felt like vomiting.

Before I knew it he was standing in front of me, checking me over.

Here it comes, I thought. *This is the day he pushes too hard.*

He glanced down at my boots, which shone like glass. Then his face soured and he knelt out of my line of vision. I could feel him scratching his fingernail across the toe of my boot to see if I had coated them in floor wax. As he did this I fought off the urge to ask him if he'd be up for giving me a hummer.

He stood up, looked at either side of my face, no doubt checking for a stray whisker. Then there was a pause that was deliberately too long before he grunted, "Better." He moved to the next man, a second later he began yelling at him.

Inspection ended and the day dragged out. I put in my time, but I was dreading going home to face Sarah. All we were going to do was argue. After last parade, I waited for Randall to head out to his car so that he wouldn't bother me during my count.

———————

Pick em and put em down... 24...25...26

I marched on, drowning out the insanity. That is why I counted, to keep my mind off the things that were driving me crazy. I needed to keep the mad demons inside my head at bay. I knew I was going insane, just barely holding on, in fact. I tried not to think about it, instead counting paces, blocking the demands, but it was only a matter of time.

I slept on the couch that night. Sarah and I didn't talk; I could barely look at her knowing that she had slept with someone else. Our end was coming, there would be no salvaging our marriage—no counseling—she'd hurt me too deeply. But there was still something I had to do before tying everything up. Instead of confrontation, I polished my boots for three hours. By the time I was finished they were so shiny you could gaze into them and brush your teeth.

I fell asleep in front of the TV and dreamed of sleeping in, and being late for morning inspection. Sgt. Pierce was yelling at me while Sarah was on her knees giving him a blow job.

———————

I woke before the alarm went off and got ready for work. After a two minute warm up on the car, I was off and running. Ten minutes later, I got to the gravel lot and saw Randall's car there. I let out a sigh of relief. It isn't that I didn't like Randall, he's a nice enough guy, but all he ever talked about were his kids. All fucking five of them. I couldn't figure it out. Private Randall, who was barely living above the poverty line, kept squeaking out kids with that brainless uterus he married. I swear to God she'd shit out a kid a year. I just didn't get it.

I started the count from my parking spot, shutting the world out.

66…67…68…69

I stared down, wondering, would this be the day? It was getting closer. As I marched I could feel myself being watched. I looked up and there he was, Sgt. Pierce, a smoke dangling from his mouth. He was staring right at me, his face hanging in a grimace. I could feel his contempt even from there. I tried to ignore it, continuing my count.

144.. 145..146.

A tank rolled down the road that separated the gravel lot from the compound, its heavy tracks clacking against the paving. When it was gone, so was Pierce. For a moment I held him in my subconscious, wishing him into a fetal position, clutching his chest, trying in vain to massage the strangling in his heart.

I smiled, keeping pace, losing myself in the count, and as I approached the building something remarkable occurred.

795...796...797...

"Oh my God," I actually said aloud.

800...801...802...804...

This had never happened before...

I stopped, hand on the door. Had I lost count when I felt Pierce's steely eyes upon me? I didn't think so, but I wanted to be sure. I looked down at my watch. It was 7:20 am. Not enough time to go back.

"Fuck," I grumbled just under my breath, then opened the door and went in.

Eight minutes later we formed up and Pierce came out. He didn't bother with an inspection. Instead he briefed us on upcoming events and told us we would be doing our annual qualifications on small arms. "Starting tomorrow, we will be going to the ranges to zero weapons and warm up. By Friday I expect everyone here to qualify. So, in respect to that I am cutting your work day short at noon and giving you administration for the rest of the day. Tomorrow morning at 5 am, we will form up here and march to the ranges. The dress will be full battle order. We will eat breakfast and lunch on the ranges, so ensure you have your KFS and Canteen cups." KFS stood for: Knife Fork Spoon. Yeah, an acronym for knife fork spoon, how fucked up is that?

He continued talking, but I was too preoccupied with the walk back to the car. Would it be over 800 paces on the way back? Was this a sign? I was excited, maybe this would all be over soon. Maybe the cosmic forces were sending me a message? Or maybe I was a stunned fuck who lost count.

"Something funny, Hicks?" It was Pierce.

"No Sergeant." The smile melted away.

As promised, they cut us loose for the afternoon and I waited for Randall and everyone else to shuffle out to their cars, so I could begin counting paces. By the time I got to my parking spot the count was 810. No Pierce to distract me, I was sure that this was the sign I'd been waiting for, but I still had something to do.

When I got into the driveway, a second event occurred that solidified my belief that there were no coincidences and that my destiny was being guided. Through the window I saw movement in the house and knew it is what I had been waiting for. I calmly parked the car and walked around to the trunk and to remove my trusty pal "Mr. Tire Iron." I then made my way to the front door and whispered. "Mr. Tire Iron, I am about to introduce you to Mr. Lover." I also decided that I would count the paces until I got him.

"Sarah, I'm home." The door swung open and then I deliberately slammed it, clicking the dead bolt over. "Sarah?"

1 ... 2 ... 3 ... 4

"I got the rest of the day off, I'm going to the rifle ranges tomorrow."

7..8

I stopped, gazed at our bedroom door, saw it was slightly open. I turned, scanning the room and then I saw it. Just the toe of a sneaker sticking out from behind the entrance to the living room.

11...12...

At the last minute he must have felt me coming, because he bolted. Unfortunately for him, I had already brought the lug wrench up over my head and was hot on his heels. I could hear him breathing, swore I heard his heart beating and then, as his fingers grazed the door knob, I heard the paces: 14...15...16 —followed by:

Thunk!

He hit the floor with a thud and blood began to pour out of the back of his head. I leaned over him, worried I might have killed him. I didn't want that. He was still alive, but I'd have to get a dressing on that wound.

Three hours later he came to. I'd tied him to a chair and once he began to come around I sat down right in front of him. I smiled, feeling power. In my hand I held a steak knife. A present from Sarah's daddy.

"Okay, here's the deal, man. I am going to take the tape off your mouth, but if you cry out I am going to drive this right into your eye and remove it. So you gotta stay calm. Think you can do that?"

He let out a sigh and nodded. I removed the tape from his mouth.

"What's your name?"

"Rick."

"Was she worth it, Rick?"

He started to cry. "You fucking killed her."

"No Rick, I didn't kill her. You killed her when you started sleeping with her."

"You sick fuck!"

"Yeah, I'm a sick fuck. Only question is what to do with you?"

His eyes widened. Suddenly self-preservation had taken a front seat. In Rick's world, Sarah had become irrelevant. Amused, I wondered how she would have reacted to that? Smiling, I picked up the tire iron and raised it.

"Now wait a minute, Mike."

"Lights out, Rick." I hit him again.

I went to work and spent about two hours getting him sorted out. When I was done I checked my work, made sure everything was tight and secure. Then I went down in the basement to prep all my kit for the next day. Preparation took a couple hours. I got my battle order all ready for the critical eye of Sgt. Pierce. Shit, I even polished my motherfucking knife fork and spoon.

After that, I laid down and woke up just after midnight when I heard the muffled cries from the bedroom. Rick was awake. I made a cup of coffee, lit a cigarette and took care of my last bit of business. I grabbed the journal you are now reading and began writing all this down.

———————

The sun will be up soon, I've loaded my gear into the car and even poked my head in the bedroom to say goodbye to Rick. While he was asleep, I stripped away his clothing and bound him to the bed where he took liberty with my wife. Then I set about binding Sarah's lifeless naked body atop his, binding their wrists and ankles together with zip ties.

Straddling him, she looked like some grotesque zombie lover gone wild. Her head caved in on one side, her left eye bloated and filled with fluid. How many times had I hit her in that last confrontation? "They should find you by noon, Rick. I thought that this would be a more fitting way to punish you for destroying my marriage. She's yours now."

His muffled cries were weak, convulsive, I hoped he wouldn't vomit through the gag and choke to death. I didn't want him to die, I wanted him to live a very long life and remember this day.

I closed the door.

I expect Rick will be pretty screwed up when this is over. While he slept I went downstairs and got the 5.56 ball ammo I had been stockpiling, and loaded up my mags.

Everything is set now.

I'm going to count the paces on the way to the ranges, and when I hit the right number...

I'm going to kill Sgt. Pierce first.

I wonder how many of them I can take out before they bring me down.

————————

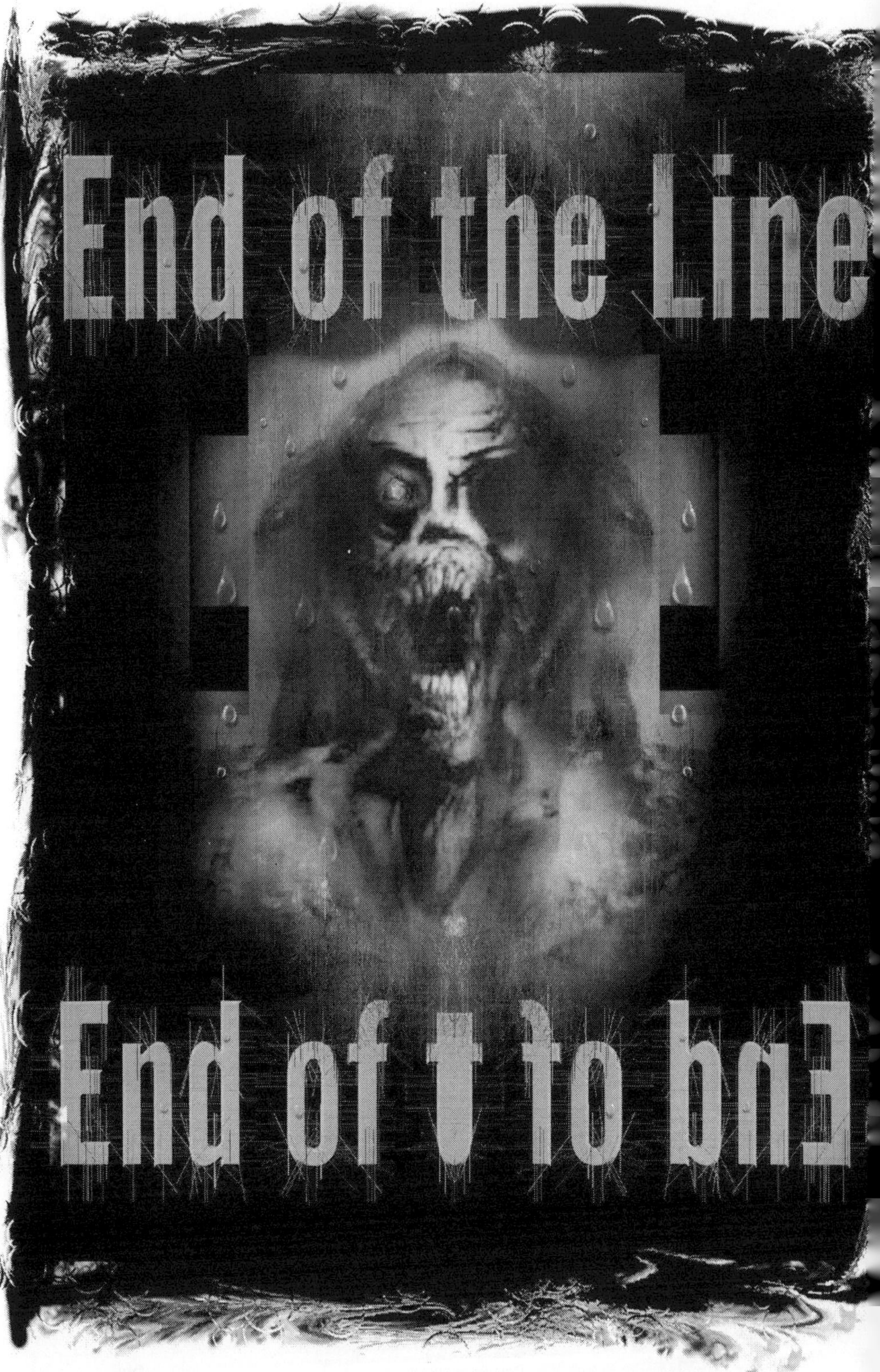
End of the Line

End of the Line

"Hand the cash over, old man!" Jimmy waved his gun about like an idiot. "Just give us the fucking cash and no one gets hurt!" He was such a fidgety guy, bouncing around. A fucking tweeker! That's all he really was and with two goddamned speeds: full throttle and stop. Franklin wondered how he'd hooked up with a fucking meth junkie, why he kept him around at all. Watching him swing that gun around, pistoling it to exclaim his point made him dangerous. He was the bad cop to Franklin's good.

"Calm down." Franklin said to Jimmy, and stepped forward. He addressed the old man, his voice calm and business-like. "Look, all we want is the cash, you grab that for us and we're gone."

The old man turned his frightened eyes from Jimmy to Franklin. "I ain't got much. Maybe hundred dollars in the register." He pushed the button on the ancient thing and it gave a ring, the change inside shuffling as the drawer sprung open.

Franklin grinned. "Come on, old fella, I know you've got a stash somewhere."

"No," the old fella said. "I ain't, made a bank deposit yesterday. We don't get a whole lotta folks out this way. There's maybe a bit more than a hundred and that's just my float."

"Look, I know you got more cash than this. Now let's just quit with…"

"You heard him!" Jimmy lunged past Franklin shoving his gun forward. "Get the fucking cash or…" —and then the gun went off, making his unfinished threat a reality. He hadn't even said it. Hadn't even spat out the second half of that sentence. His ears popped, contracting defensively against the assault of exploding gunpowder.

What happened? How? How?

The back of the old man's head burst like a water balloon. Brain matter, peppered with bone splashed against the wall. And rather than falling, the old man hung there, suspended by some imaginary force. The bullet caught him just below the right eye, a black dot not much bigger than a pencil eraser, darkening a half an inch below the rim of his weathered eye socket. The imaginary puppet strings which held his dead body upright dissolved and he dropped to the floor. It wasn't like in the movies. The bullet from the gun did not throw the old man back, it just went through him and popped the back of his head.

"You fucking idiot." He could barely hear himself above the ringing in his ears. There was no time to think, he grabbed the cash from the open register drawer then snagged Jimmy by the arm and dragged him out of the store.

Jimmy was in shock, still trying to process what had just happened. Staring at the gun, then back at the store. The passenger door opened and he stared numbly. He'd never actually killed anyone before. It was unreal, like a crazy dream. Inside his head, a pressure steam whistle drowned out everything around him, even Franklin. He barely heard him yelling. "Get in the car, Jimmy! We gotta fucking ride!"

"Oh my God!" Jimmy screamed. "I didn't mean it. The gun… It just went off!"

"Shut up!" Franklin growled, jamming the shifter in gear and tromping on the gas. From beneath the rear wheels of the Olds 88, gravel spat high into the air as they sped from the lot. Franklin never said a word, he stared ahead, focused only on the getaway. His heart pounded. He was pissed and needed every ounce of self-control to keep from pulling over and pistol whipping Jimmy into unconsciousness. He gazed into the rear-view mirror, back toward the dust cloud. They were on asphalt now, but they needed to make some distance. He would deal with Jimmy later, when they'd put some space between themselves and that country store.

Gotta hit the highway, before someone wanders into that store.

An hour later they were sixty miles away and he had calmed down somewhat. While Jimmy looked out the passenger window, Franklin considered his situation. Up until this day he'd never done anything worse than armed robbery. They were in the big time now and if he went before a judge it would be the end. He focused on the road looking for cop cars. Ahead, the mountains invited escape. The big car, destined for extinction, was left to Franklin by his Mother after she died. It was a pig on gas, but suitable for making fast getaways from the odd burglary or stick up. Up to this point there hadn't been any complications.

Franklin pushed down on the accelerator, the big Olds lunged forward—climbing the hill with all its might. Beside him, Jimmy fidgeted, knowing that when the car came to a stop they would pony up the cash and if he was lucky Franklin would just knock him around a bit. He hadn't intended on killing the old man, the gun just went off. He didn't even squeeze the trigger, he was waving it around and it went off. He wondered how he would reason that with Franklin. To make matters worse, the take looked to be pretty low budget.

They drove on for two more hours winding through the mountains, daylight giving way to dusk and the eventual dark. While Franklin gripped the wheel tight, steering through bends and turns, Jimmy nodded in and out of sleep. That's what Jimmy did when things got tense. He slept and it irritated the living shit out of Franklin.

The stupid fucker shoots an old man in the face and then grabs himself a cat nap.

Up ahead he saw a sign and figured they were far enough out now that a police pursuit wasn't in the cards. He clicked on the high beams and began slowing down for the overlook which stretched out across the south side of the mountain. Across from the lonely highway over the expanse of a 3000 foot gorge, a single railroad track mirrored their route. On it a train moved silently along, looking like a toy, so small and quiet.

Franklin put the car in park.

"Get up." He gave Jimmy a push. "We've got business."

Jimmy opened his eyes and saw Franklin's leaning in the driver door, the interior light blinded him to the night. "Where are we?"

"We're in a rest area. Come on out and grab a piss if you need one then we'll divvy up the take." Franklin closed the door and the interior light shut off. Jimmy watched him move around to the front of the car and lay his gun and the small bag of money down on the hood of the Eighty-Eight.

Jimmy was scared and rightly so. He got out of the car and headed over to a bush to take a leak when Franklin called from behind him. "Jimmy, this will only take a minute. Come over here and you can grab a quick piss before we head down the road."

He turned around and walked back to the car, his heart sinking in his chest. *He doesn't seem mad. Maybe he's over it,* he tried to reassure himself, but knew better.

Franklin didn't get riled up—he just acted. Back in Terrisdale Prison, a couple goons were trying to muscle him in the shower. Franklin didn't show an ounce of emotion, what he did was listen and nod as the lead goon, a mean looking mass of tattoo and muscle told him how it was gonna be. Franklin appeared intent on taking the lead goon's crap, but he was actually sizing him up. Before the Q&A was over Franklin had beat the leader into a bloody pulp. As the deposed leader lay dying on the shower floor, lifeblood swirling down the drain, Franklin turned to one of the two accomplices.

"You want to work for me or join your friend?"

Accomplice one looked at the battered naked body on the floor and nodded. "I'm looking for work."

"What about you," Franklin said, looking Jimmy's direction. "You in or out?"

Jimmy was by the door. Goon number three had blocked the exit until the bloody carcass, formerly known as goon number one, was done tuning up Franklin and showing him who the boss of C Block was.

Goon number three said, "I'm in…"

"Not you. Him." Franklin pointed toward Jimmy. "You."

"Me," Jimmy asked.

"Yeah, you want a job?"

"Sure."

Jimmy had been up on break and enter. Multiple break and enters was more like it, he'd burglarized four apartments looking for drugs and money to feed his glass habit. Looking back on it he couldn't believe how stupid he'd been. He'd hit the same building three times and had begun to feel sort of invincible on his third visit. So when the apartment didn't have much to offer he decided to check out the one next door. He was rifling through the medicine cabinet when the cops walked in. He was sentenced to two years less a day, which kept him out of a Federal Prison. He was already a year into his sentence when he and Franklin met that fateful afternoon. He served less than 13 months and was paroled from Terrisdale the same day Franklin's conviction was overturned. That was two months ago and four jobs ago. He hit the pipe a week after getting out and the jitters took over.

Now he'd killed a man.

"Come on, Jimmy, we haven't got all day," Franklin said bringing him back. Behind him the sky was jet blue as night encroached, and the locomotive too far away to hear kept chugging along, smoke puffing from its back, pulling its endless line of freight cars through the mountains. Franklin was just a silhouette—dark daunting—no emotion. He was a big man, six foot three, shoulder length hair and chiseled features that were undoubtedly Native American. "Let's get this split done and we'll hit the road."

"Uhh, okay." Jimmy felt his bladder contract, and a nervous squirt of urine dribbled down his leg. He would have to wait, but he hoped that Franklin didn't because he would definitely piss his pants. He walked back to the fender of the car and stood across from him. Franklin held the gun in his left, pressing it sideways against the battered hood of the Olds. In his right hand he held the take from the robbery.

He pushed the bag across the hood never faltering the gun's muzzle which was pointed straight across at Jimmy. "Put your gun on the hood and count the money, Jimmy."

Slowly, Jimmy pulled out his gun and placed it on the hood of the car, then reluctantly reached across and took the bag from Franklin. His hand grazed Franklin's finger and he began to feel hopeless.

"Count out loud, two piles." Franklin's voice was cool and dangerous.

"I didn't mean…"

"Shut up and count."

"Okay," Jimmy croaked and began to count out loud. It didn't take long and when he was finished making two piles they stood there in the darkness across from each other two small stacks of money laid out.

"One hundred and twenty-seven bucks," Franklin finally said. "That's what you shot that old guy in the face for—a lousy hundred and twenty-seven bucks.

"Look Franklin, I didn't......" Jimmy started.

"Shut up." Franklin raised his eyes from the hood. "You think I give a shit about some old man?" He grinned.

Jimmy would have relaxed, but knew better. "It was an accident Franklin."

"You're an accident Jimmy. I don't give a rat's ass about some old man, but now they're going to be looking for us and your gun. We have to get rid of it."

He said we! I'm gonna be okay.

"We gotta dump that gun and get as far away from here as possible. Grab some napkins from inside the car to wipe it down." Franklin unloaded Jimmy's gun as he went back to get the serviettes from the glove box.

When he returned, Franklin handed the gun across to him and using the napkins he wiped it down while using another napkin to hold it by the barrel. When he was done he looked to Franklin and said, "Now what?"

"Toss it into the gorge." He pointed to the guardrail at the edge of the parking area.

Jimmy ambled away from Franklin, not wanting to look back, terrified that this would be the end. When he reached the guardrail, he gazed out across the gorge wondering how often anyone came around and if there were any trails down there.

"Throw it as far as you can, Jimmy." Franklin called from behind him.

He cocked his arm back and threw as hard as he could. It spun outward, breaking free of the napkin which fluttered in the upward draft. The gun disappeared into the blackness, and though he listened, he never heard it hit bottom.

He then turned to see Franklin standing behind him, gun raised. "End of the line, Jimmy."

"No! Please, Franklin."

"You're a liability now, I can't keep you around anymore. I should have known better than to hook up with a tweeker in the first place. I won't put that on you. Nope, that one is my fault. I take full responsibility for that one." Franklin cocked the hammer back.

"Come on, man. Please. I don't wanna die." Jimmy was blubbering now.

"You remember what I told you? I said it when you picked up that glass pipe."

Jimmy stared incredulously. He remembered, and he could hear the warning he should have heeded. When he caught him smoking again. He was in a rest area bathroom and after Franklin kicked in the stall door, snatched the pipe from his hand, he said, "If you can't take care of business, you got no business doing that shit."

"Franklin, please!"

"I'll give you a choice. You can jump or I'll shoot you."

"Goddamn it, no. Please! I'm sorry."

"I can't trust you, Jimmy. You get picked up somewhere and talk to the cops, I'm done. You're a liability now. I cannot risk it." Franklin brought the gun up ready to shoot. "End of the line."

Jimmy turned then, knowing that if he didn't jump Franklin would shoot him where he stood and toss him over.

Maybe I can grab something on the way down and stop myself. He was up on the guardrail now teetering back and forth. The gorge swirled below, a bottomless black hole. Across the chasm the train continued its silent trek. He was building his nerve when he heard two words.

"Times up." Franklin said from behind him, and pulled the trigger.

The report from the gun was swallowed by the darkness and the bullet, when it hit him, felt more like a pinch. Then he was tumbling downward into the abysmal dark. He never saw the rock outcropping when he smashed against it. There was a thud—

crunch of compressing vertebrae—splintering of bone, and then fade to black.

Franklin walked slowly to the edge, gun at the ready to fire if necessary, but Jimmy was gone. Swallowed in the darkness. Remorse began to creep in, but not for Jimmy. He thought that maybe he should have waited and buried his body. If a hiker came across the body, they would connect Jimmy to him.

Then from behind him there was laughter.

He spun around, ready to shoot and saw the silhouette standing by the car watching him. He felt a sudden pang of alarm. The figure was tall, even taller than Franklin himself.

"Who's there?"

"Who's there?" The dark figure parroted.

"I'm not fucking around!" He marched toward the car, gun up ready to open up if necessary. He couldn't make out the dark figure. Could only see his eyes, which gave off a silvery glint. When he was ten feet away, he realized the sheer height of the stranger. He stood over seven feet. He was a fucking giant.

Where did he come from? There's no car.

"Who are you," Franklin asked.

"What is your name?" The stranger asked.

"Wouldn't you like to know," he scoffed. "Just step away from my car."

"Car, is that what you call this?" The man then scraped his nails across the hood.

"I mean it! Step off or I'll shoot you in the head."

"Go ahead," the man said and then there was a blur in his reality.

Franklin looked to his right hand and the gun was gone.

The silhouette was now standing on the roof of the Olds holding Franklin's gun up in one hand. He—no—it tossed the gun into the darkness, until it somewhere off in the distance and then the stranger turned his attention back on Franklin.

"What the... How did?"

"Look at me." The silver in the stranger's eyes began to swirl, turning his eyes into shiny mercury-filled globes. Franklin felt himself being drawn into the hypnotic pull of those eyes, felt himself losing control and felt it probing into his mind. "Tell me your name."

"Franklin," he said feeling suddenly sleepy.

"Come closer, I want to show you something."

"Who are you?"

"I am as old as time, and until tonight I have had no name. At least not one I liked." It climbed down from the roof, and onto the hood of the Old. Now it was eight feet tall, long and lanky, arms unfurling into appendages that carried hooked talons.

There was a smell, one of rot and death.

Franklin felt himself sleepwalking forward. He was being anesthetized by those chromium eyes. He could not resist, nor did he want to. The incident with Jimmy seemed a thousand years ago. He wanted to stay like this forever.

Does it feel good, Franklin, the voice inside his head asked.

"Yes, good." He was swimming in euphoria, standing below the stranger, not knowing or caring where it had come from or what it was. He supposed this was how Jimmy felt when he sucked up the steady burn of glass. This was bliss. Calming steady waves of love.

Yes, that is what it is. Love. I feel love.

He did not see the gaunt creature hunched over him, the grey translucent skin reflecting in the starlight. Nor did he see the rotted teeth or the black ick spilling from its mouth in yolky tendrils. "I like your name," it soothed. "Franklin."

"Thank you."

"Can I have it?"

"What? My name?"

"Yes."

"My gift to you," he murmured. He was locked in the contemplation of its chromium eyes, lost in the mirrors of its eternal darkness. He did not see the talons digging into the hood of his Olds, or see the creature lift its foot the incisor toe, a jagged talon, lifting as it took on a striking posture, ready to disembowel. He felt only love and warmth. Far off he heard its waking voice. "Franklin?"

"Yes."

"Open your eyes."

He did not want to. He wanted to stay in this state forever, but the anesthesia was wearing off. He tried to hold on, to grip the rocks of this oceanic bliss but the tides pulled the waters away. The cool night air was returning, he was coming down.

He opened his eyes then and saw Jimmy standing over him.

"End of the line, Franklin," The thing that was Jimmy said.

Terror cut into him.

"There we go," it said through jagged tombstone teeth. Then Jimmy began to change, and he—It turned up to the star-filled sky and let out a horrific shriek that spiraled out in ear shattering octaves and echoed across the gorge.

"Noooooo," Franklin screamed and tried to pull away.

And then felt his belly light on fire as it sliced through him. Fireflies of pain lit inside his abdomen. What had it done to him?

His chin dropped to his chest. He saw talons pulling out great handfuls of his insides. Then he became numb, and still there were ripping sounds. Tearing of flesh, liquid ropey gluts of blood plopping downward, pattering upon the asphalt. He fell from its grasp, bleeding out, slipping away and it was on him, digging and tearing.

It gorged, emptying the belly of the man, feeding the unending hunger—pausing only to let a second nightmarish shriek loose upon the night. Then it returned to the feed, pulling a fresh clutch of entrails, gulping obsessively, trying to sate the insatiable hunger that plagued it. When it was finished it dumped his hollow carcass into the gorge, the same spot where the spoiled meat had been dropped. Then it pushed the car down the bank, to the opening it had made. It went crashing down through the trees into the darkness and was gone.

Oh well, it had a new name and for now its hunger was sated.

The creature changed form and flew up into the night.

———————

Jimmy opened his good eye, the one that had not exploded when he landed on the rock shelf, to see Franklin's dead eyes staring back—wide open—full of terror. He could not speak, his larynx was crushed and was barely holding on, in fact. He was dying. He knew that he was not long for this earth. *What had thrown Franklin from the edge,* he wondered. *And what had thrown the others?*

There were so many.
So many bones.

———

Afterword

In between my bigger projects I can sometimes be found dabbling in the world of short stories. I have always been in awe of the constant short story writer. There are so many out there who do it so well and are so damned prolific. Back in the 1980's, I was a voracious reader of dark fiction. I regularly poked my nose into full length novels, but also found myself a regular reader of short fiction from writers like Robert R. McCammon, Ramsey Campbell, John Skipp, and even Harlan Ellison. These fantastic writers could be found in all sorts of print, but there were a number of magazines where you could get a glimpse into their world.

Two of my personal favorites were Twilight Zone and Night Cry Magazine. These magazines were a constant companion; carried with me even when I was in the army. Sometimes, I'd be in a trench puffing away on a smoke, leaning over a machine gun with the magazine spread out. This was something my superiors weren't too keen on, but I didn't care. I was immersed in an excerpt from Robert R. McCammon's Apocalyptic Opus: Swan Song or I was reading something by the late great Rod Serling.

While most soldiers had a stack of Penthouse magazines, I had a pile of Twilight Zone and Night Cry. This raised questions about my masculinity—that died off when they caught a glimpse of the girl I was engaged to marry—only to be replaced by the consensus that I was weird.

I used to write short stories quite regularly, but over the years, many of them, the truly magical ones, have been lost. Among them were a bunch of post-apocalyptic tales inspired by films like Planet of the Apes, The Omega Man, and Damnation Alley.

These are stories that involved modern day crucifixion, nuclear war and giant insects. Someday, if time permits, I may reach back into the grey matter and see if I can resurrect some of that magic.

M.j. Preston

Publishing Credits

RUN-OFF 31 – Originally published in Canopic Jars: Tales of Mummies and Mummification. Available from Great Old Ones Publishing.

Revelation Lamb – Originally published as a Kindle Short with my self-proprietorship Skinwalker Press.

Passion – Originally published in the **now defunct** Dark Passages Magazine. But the ghost of that project lives on and inspired this collection.

The Children of Romani Phoneutria – Was published in Bugs: Tales that Sliver, Creep and Crawl. Available from Great Old Ones Publishing.

Counting Paces – Was presented as an audio presentation on the online Podcast: Tales to Terrify.

End of the Line – Published in two parts as Skin: End of the line in the Fanzine: SUMMERLANDS, as an illustrated story. Artwork by Ogmios the Artist.

ABOUT THE AUTHOR

M.J. Preston hails from Canada, where he pursues writing fiction, creating digital art and dabbling in photography. He is the author of the novels: The Equinox, Acadia Event and his stories and artwork can be found in various anthologies and fanzines.

In 2016, he will be releasing his third novel, **Highwayman—The Black Highway Book 1** and is now working on the sequel, **4 —The Black Highway Book 2.**

To learn more about M.J. Preston visit him on the internet at: http://mjpreston.net

Dear Reader,

Hey, it's me again.

Just a friendly reminder, that if you enjoyed this collection please leave a review. Unlike large publishing houses, independent artists do not have the luxury of an expensive marketing team, so your input is instrumental in keeping independent art alive.

At present independent artists around the world are struggling to bring their art to the public eye. They do not do this simply for monetary gain, but to share their creations with others.

If you like an artist's work, please, tell others and buy their work so that the artist can continue to create.

Thank you for your support.

M.J. PRESTON

More From M.J. Preston

ACADIA EVENT

Author M.J. Preston creates an epic page-turner, with Canada's frozen north as the setting and the Earth as the ultimate prize for whichever side wins the war. – Gregory L. Norris, Screenwriter, Star trek Voyager

In 2012 and 2013, Author, M.J. Preston set out to run the world's longest Ice Road. Now he's returned with the much anticipated novel Acadia Event. Marty Croft has it all. A beautiful wife and a successful career as a commercial artist. However, he has a secret and it has come back to haunt him. Enter Gordon Shamus. Gordon is a psychopath with a short fuse who won't take "no" for an answer. Forced back into a world he thought he had left behind Marty heads to the ice roads of Canada to do one last heist. In a twist of fate, that becomes least of his worries. At the Acadia Diamond Mine, they have made a major discovery. Something buried in the ice, not of this world and it is about to be unleashed.

Available in both print and digital format at sellers like Amazon, Barnes and Noble and for order at your local library.

To learn more visit: hrttp://mjpreston.net

THE EQUINOX

When a tribe of native people in the Northwest Territories of Canada are snowed in from the world, they are forced to resort to inhuman ways of survival. When a presence is drawn to their suffering, an evil blankets their continued existence until a misfortunate occurrence results in the spread of the terror to more populated lands. With its ensemble cast, the novel takes paths that lead to a serial killer, demonic monsters, and a police department that slowly discovers that there may be something deeper into the crimes that have transpired in their small farming town in Manitoba.

SUPPORT INDEPENDENT PRESS

Manufactured by Amazon.ca
Bolton, ON

34328636R00074